Witch Is Where Magic Lives Now

Published by Implode Publishing Ltd
© Implode Publishing Ltd 2020

Chapter 1

(Author's note: This is the first book of season four. It picks up the story SIX YEARS after the previous book)

"Mrs V!" I had to shout in order to be heard over the noise of the vacuum cleaner.

"Sorry, dear?" She turned it off.

"The office is fine now, honestly. You don't need to do any more cleaning."

"I just want to do another dust over in that corner." She grabbed the feather duster, went over to the filing cabinet and began to give it the once (or, as it turned out, the twice) over.

Ever since I'd told Mrs V that I was expecting a visit from Lady Tweaking, she'd been like a woman possessed: Vacuuming here, vacuuming there. Tidying here, tidying there. Dusting here, dusting everywhere.

"Honestly, Mrs V, the office looks fine now."

"Alright dear. I'll just get out the best cups and give them a wash."

"*Best cups*? I didn't realise we had any *best* cups."

"I keep them for special occasions."

"I don't think I've ever seen them, have I?"

"Probably not. I'm not sure they've been out since your father died, but you can't expect Lady Tweaking to drink out of those horrible mugs that you normally use, can you?"

"Err—no, I suppose not. Where do you keep these best cups?"

"In my super-secret drawer."

"Where's your *super-secret* drawer?"

"In my super-secret filing cabinet."

"I didn't know you had a *super-secret* filing cabinet."

"That's because it's —"

"*Super-secret*. I get it."

Mrs V glanced over at Winky, who was lying on the sofa, watching all the comings and goings. "What about him?"

"Winky? What about him?"

"What kind of impression will it give her ladyship when she sees him? Cats do not belong in the office environment. Shall I throw him outside for a while?"

I glanced out of the window; it was pouring with rain. "You can't do that, he'll get soaked. I'll make sure he stays out of sight, under the sofa."

"Very well. I'll go and wash the best cups."

"The old bag lady has finally lost it, wouldn't you say?" Winky commented when Mrs V had left the room. "Super-secret drawers in super-secret filing cabinets? The woman is clearly nuts. You should get her locked up in some super-secret padded cell and throw away the super-secret key."

"She's only trying to help. I have a prospective client arriving shortly."

"Lady what's-her-face? So what?"

"Mrs V is doing everything she can to make sure we make a good impression on her ladyship."

"Shouldn't *you* be the one doing that?"

"I can't see the point. I've always believed people should take me as they find me, regardless of who they are."

"I can see that course you went on recently did you the power of good. What was it called again?"

"Developing a customer-focussed business."

"That was it." He laughed. "Is that attitude something they taught you on the course?"

"That course was a waste of time—they always are. I only went on it because Kathy twisted my arm. She said it helped her to grow her business."

"Sounds like another epic fail to me."

"Just make sure when Lady Tweaking arrives that you stay out of sight, under the sofa. Understood?"

"What's it worth?"

"I'll tell you what it's worth. It's worth not being thrown outside in the rain."

Fifteen minutes later, Lady Tweaking arrived.

"This way, your ladyship," Mrs V said in her Sunday-best voice. "Can I get you a drink? Tea? Coffee?"

"Tea would be splendid. Thank you."

"We have biscuits too if you'd care for one."

"Just the tea, please. A splash of milk, but no sugar."

"Very well, your ladyship." Mrs V practically curtsied as she backed out of the room.

Lady Tweaking wasn't exactly what I'd been expecting. I'd assumed she'd be wearing designer clothes and lots of jewellery. Instead, she looked like a bag of rags tied round the middle, more charity chic than designer. In her late sixties, she had thinning grey hair and was wearing no makeup whatsoever.

"Mrs Maxwell, I assume?" Her firm handshake belied her frail frame.

"That's right, but there's no need for formalities. Please call me Jill."

"And you may call me Caroline."

"Caroline? I couldn't possibly do that. It would feel disrespectful, your ladyship."

"None of this 'your ladyship' nonsense either."

"Sorry, I don't understand."

"The title isn't real."

"But I thought —"

"My ancestors have owned Tweaking Manor for centuries. Over that time, the locals have always referred to the owners as the lord and lady of the manor, but there's no basis in law for them to do so. Some of my predecessors revelled in the title, but frankly I find it rather embarrassing, so Caroline will do nicely."

"I see. Caroline it is, then."

Lady Tweaking took a moment to study her surroundings and, if her expression was anything to go by, she was none too impressed.

By way of a distraction, I said, "I believe we're neighbours, Lady — err — Caroline."

"*Neighbours?* Really?"

"We moved into the old watermill a couple of months ago."

"I'm not sure I know it."

"It's in Middle Tweaking."

"Oh yes. I remember now. Didn't that Turtle woman used to live there?"

"Myrtle, yes she did. She moved to the coast about six years ago."

"I thought it was strange that I hadn't heard from her in a while. She had a bad habit of sticking her nose where it wasn't wanted. Tell me, Jill, are you familiar with Tweaking Manor?"

"Only in as much as I've driven past it several times. That's all."

Mrs V came in with the tea. "Is there enough milk in there for you, your ladyship?"

"Yes, that's splendid. Thank you."

I did a double take at the china cups.

After Mrs V had left us alone, Winky came out from under the sofa and jumped onto the windowsill.

Memo to self: Kill him later.

"I see you have a cat." Caroline looked up from her tea.

"Err, yes."

"He only has one eye."

"That's right. His name is Winky."

"I have a few cats of my own; five at the last count. Although, Arthur probably won't be with us for much longer."

"I'm sorry to hear that. Is he very old?"

"No. Barely more than a kitten. He's too lively for me so I've found him a good home with a friend of mine: Lorna Warner. You probably know her."

"I don't think so."

"You must do. She's one of the Sussex Warners."

"Oh, right. The Sussex Warners." I had no idea who she was talking about. "Of course."

"Your young man looks full of life too." She gestured towards Winky.

"Too much sometimes. So, Caroline, what is it that I can do for you?"

"Some blighter has stolen the Tweaking Goblet."

"From Tweaking Manor? Is it very valuable?"

"Not particularly. It is silver, but it's quite small. I doubt it would fetch much as scrap, and you certainly wouldn't find a buyer for it as it is. Between you and me, it's an ugly thing, but it has been in the family for centuries and is rich with tradition."

"Oh?"

"As the estate passes from one generation to the next, the name of the new owner is engraved on the goblet. The thought that it should disappear on my watch is simply unbearable."

"And you say it went missing from Tweaking Manor? Where exactly was it kept?"

"In the games room."

"Is that room normally locked?"

"No, it has never seemed necessary."

"Was there a break-in? Was anything else stolen?"

"There are no signs of a break-in and as far as I can ascertain, nothing else seems to be missing. Just the goblet."

"Have you contacted the police?"

"No. I'd prefer to keep them out of this if I can. Our family likes to maintain a low profile. If people were to see police cars milling around the manor, well, you know how they gossip."

"I understand. If the goblet isn't valuable, can you think of any other reason why someone might want to take it?"

"No, I can't. I've racked my brain, but I haven't come up with a single reason. It doesn't make any sense."

"When was it taken?"

"It must have happened sometime between midnight on Wednesday and six o'clock on Thursday morning. That's when I noticed that it had gone.

"And you're positive it was there on Wednesday at midnight?"

"Absolutely. I was up much later than usual that night because we'd had a family gathering. It was my birthday."

"Not the best of birthday presents."

"Indeed. To be honest, at my age, I'd prefer not to celebrate my birthday, but the family insisted, so I was forced to go along with it."

"And you went into the games room before you retired for the night?"

"Yes. I'd told Mulgrave he could call it a day at ten o'clock. He normally finishes after dinner at about seven, but I'd asked him to work later that night. After everyone had left, I checked all the rooms downstairs before retiring to bed. Just to make sure the lights were out—that kind of thing. The goblet was definitely in the games room then."

"Who is Mulgrave?"

"My butler."

"Who was at your birthday party?"

"It was hardly a party. Just a dinner for the family: My brother, my sister, and my son and his wife. That was pretty much it, really."

"Was there anyone else in the manor at the time? Apart from Mulgrave?"

"Mrs Jones was there, but she'd gone by ten too."

"Who's she?"

"The cook."

"Do both she and Mulgrave live on the premises?"

"Mulgrave does. Mrs Jones lives in Lower Tweaking. I've known them for many years—they're both extremely trustworthy. I can't believe they had anything to do with the theft."

"Where is Mulgrave's room?"

"In the east wing. It's the only room that hasn't been boarded up in that wing."

"Does he spend most of his time at the house?"

"Yes. He doesn't have any relatives as far as I can make out. Or friends. He seems to prefer his own company. The only time he goes out, other than to run errands for me, is when he takes his evening walk."

"Into the village?"

"No. He usually just walks around the grounds. He must be a hardy soul because he does it in all weathers. So, tell me, Jill, do you think you'll be able to help us to find the goblet?"

"I'll do my best. I will need to pay a visit to Tweaking Manor. I assume that's okay?"

"Yes, provided you don't turn up in a car with flashing lights and a siren."

"Could we possibly arrange my visit now? How about this afternoon?"

"I'm afraid I'm busy for the rest of the day. I have lunch with the Leadbeaters and those usually stretch out for the whole afternoon."

"What about tomorrow?"

She took a diary from her handbag. "I'm tied up in the afternoon, but I'm free all morning."

"Great. I'll pop over first thing if that's okay. I'd like to take a good look around the games room, and perhaps have a brief look around the rest of the house too."

"That's fine."

"Also, if you could prepare a list of names and contact details for all the people who were at the birthday dinner.

That would be really helpful."

"I'll have that waiting for you." She stood up. "Right, if there's nothing else, I must be making tracks." On her way out, she walked over to Winky, and gave him a little scratch under the chin. "What a handsome boy you are. And so brave with just the one eye."

As soon as Caroline was out of the door, Winky said, "I thought she was supposed to be rolling in it. She looked like she'd been sleeping rough."

"That's a little harsh." True, though.

"I reckon you owe me a tin of salmon."

"For what?"

"Didn't you see the expression on her face when she first saw your office? She was clearly not impressed, but then she spotted me, and her attitude changed. If you ask me, I'm the only reason you got this case."

Mrs V came into my office.

"How did it go with her ladyship, Jill? Was she impressed?"

"She must have been because she's given me the case. She looked a little rough, don't you think?"

"Not at all. I thought she looked quite sophisticated."

"She looked like a bag of rags."

"Jill! You really mustn't speak about her ladyship like that. Just because you don't understand the fashion sense of the upper classes, doesn't mean you should criticise." Mrs V noticed Winky on the windowsill. "I thought he was going to stay under the sofa."

"It's okay. It seems that Caroline is quite fond of cats."

"Caroline?" Mrs V looked horrified. "You can't call her

ladyship by her first name."

"She isn't actually a lady."

"Jill!"

"I mean the title isn't real. She told me so herself. She prefers to be called Caroline."

"Really? And to think I brought out the best cups."

"She seems quite nice. Very down to earth."

"Hmm." Mrs V was clearly unimpressed. "While you were with *Caroline*, there's been some coming and going down the corridor."

"In Clowns' old offices?"

"Yes. It looks like someone might be moving in."

"I didn't think they were ever going to let that place again. How long has it been now since Jimmy and Kimmy moved out?"

"It must be almost eighteen months."

"Any idea who's moving in?"

"No. I couldn't tell from the boxes, but I'll keep my ear to the ground."

***

Aunt Lucy had been a little poorly over the weekend, so yesterday she'd contacted me to ask if I'd pop over this morning to take Barry for a walk.

When I magicked myself over to her house, I was surprised to find her in the kitchen, tidying the cupboards.

"Aunt Lucy, what are you doing? You're supposed to be resting."

"Good morning, Jill. It's okay. When I woke up this morning, I felt back to my old self."

"And you decided you'd have a spring clean?"

"You know me. I like to keep busy."

"You should be resting."

"I'm not on my last legs yet. It was just a twenty-four hour bug. You're as bad as the twins. They were over here first thing this morning, to check up on me."

"I'm not checking up on you. If you remember, you asked if I'd take Barry for a walk."

"Sorry, I'd totally forgotten about that. There's no need now. I'll be fine."

We were interrupted by the sound of paws on the stairs. Moments later, Barry burst into the room, and almost knocked me off my feet.

"Jill, are we going for a walk? Please, Jill!"

"Yes, Barry."

"I love to go for a walk, Jill."

"I know you do."

"Can we go to the park? I love the park."

"Yes, Barry, we can go to the park."

"Can we go now? Please!"

"I just need a couple of minutes. Why don't you sit in the hall and wait for me?"

"Okay. Don't be long. I love the park."

"I won't be long, I promise."

"I'd like to come with you if you don't mind," Aunt Lucy said, rather sheepishly.

"You're supposed to be resting."

"I've been stuck in this house for two days and I'm going stir crazy. And besides, I could do with the fresh air. Once we're there, Barry can have a run around while we have a sit down. Please, Jill."

"Okay, but if you start to feel poorly, you must tell me, and we'll turn back."

"I promise. I'll get my coat."

We didn't have an opportunity to talk on the way to the park because Barry was pulling on the lead all the time. Once we were there, I let him loose and he ran off into the distance. We found a bench at the highest point of the park from where we could keep an eye on him. To be fair to Barry, he was pretty well behaved these days, nothing like as mischievous as he'd been when he was younger.

Famous last words.

"How's Lester's new business venture going?" I said.

"So far, so good." Aunt Lucy crossed her fingers.

"How long has the shop been open now?"

"It's three weeks today, and from what he's told me, business is improving every day."

"I'm really pleased for him. He's had more than his fair share of bad luck with jobs."

"It's all thanks to you, Jill. If you hadn't found him that job with the mobile fish man, he never would have ended up opening a shop of his own."

"And financially? Things are okay?"

"We had to stretch ourselves to find the money to open the shop, but if sales continue at the current levels, we'll be fine. The main thing is that he really loves what he's doing now. Who'd have thought his vocation was to be a fishmonger?"

Lester had opened his fishmonger's shop in West Chipping, where he'd managed to find vacant premises in the high street at a relatively low rent. I was thrilled to hear that things were going so well for him. After all the lousy jobs he'd had, he deserved a break.

"Have you heard from your grandmother recently, Jill?"

Aunt Lucy was already looking much better for being out in the fresh air.

"Not for a few days. In fact, now you mention it, I reckon it must be over a week. Why? She's okay, isn't she?"

"She's fine. I saw her yesterday and she seemed on top form. It's just that when she sold her Ever empire, I was afraid that she wouldn't be able to handle retirement. I fully expected her to be popping over to my house every five minutes, but quite the opposite. If anything, I see less of her now than when she was running all those shops."

Just under a year ago, Grandma had taken us all by surprise when she'd decided to divest herself of her Ever empire. Some of the shops had been sold. Kathy had bought ForEver Bride, Deli had purchased Ever Beauty, but there had been no buyers for Ever A Wool Moment or Ever, both of which had simply closed down.

"What do you think she's up to?" I said.

"I have no idea, and I really don't like to ask."

At that moment, Barry came running back up the park.

"What's that he's got in his mouth?" Aunt Lucy pointed.

"I'm not sure. Something red."

"Look what I found." Barry dropped the handbag at my feet.

"Where did you get that, Barry?"

"Down there."

"Yes, but whereabouts down there, exactly?"

"It was on one of these." He touched the bench with his paw.

"On a bench?"

"Yes. It's nice, isn't it? Can I keep it?"

"Was anyone sitting on the bench?"

"No. There was only this."

Moments later, a woman came running towards us. By the time she reached us she was out of breath and red in the face.

"Hey, your dog has pinched my handbag."

Oh bum!

Chapter 2

The only way I'd been able to placate the irate woman was to give her the money for a replacement handbag. I couldn't blame her for being so angry: Barry's teeth had punctured the bag in a couple of places. After I'd handed over the money, she transferred her possessions over to her shopping bag.

"He can keep that," she said.

"Are you sure?"

"It's no good to me now, is it?"

And, so it was that Barry, who was totally oblivious to the mayhem he'd caused, proudly carried it back home in his mouth.

By the time we got back to Aunt Lucy's house, she was ready to put her head down for a while, so I magicked myself over to Washbridge and headed for Coffee Animal. The shop had recently undergone a rebranding (from Coffee Games) after an unfortunate incident during pin the tail on the donkey day. The new name struck me as a little weird, but when I'd enquired about the reason for it, I'd been told all would become clear after the 'official' launch, which was scheduled for the following week.

As I walked through the door, I spotted Kathy seated at a table near the counter, so I grabbed a drink and joined her.

"I didn't expect to find you in here."

"I needed a break." She sighed. "We've been run off our feet all morning. It feels like everyone and her sister has decided to get married this year."

"You're not complaining, are you?"

"Of course not. Business is booming, and that's just the way I like it."

"By the way, when does your new shop open? It can't be long now."

"Two months tomorrow."

"That's number six, isn't it?"

"Seven if you include ForEver Bride."

"I still can't believe the deal you negotiated to buy that from Grandma. I never thought she'd take your lowball offer."

"Neither did I, but she was really keen to sell. Speaking of your grandmother, how is she? I haven't seen her for a while."

"I haven't seen much of her either, but according to Aunt Lucy, she's fine. Ever since Grandma retired, she seems to be busier than ever."

"Doing what?"

"I've no idea, and I intend to keep it that way. Let's not spoil the morning talking about her. How are the kids?"

"Much the same. Like I told you the last time I saw you, Mikey is at that age now when he considers his parents to be one big embarrassment."

"To be fair, you are quite embarrassing, Kathy."

"Thanks. You can laugh now, but your time will come. Seriously, though, Mikey and Pete seem to do nothing but argue these days."

"That's a real shame. Those two used to do loads of stuff together: Fishing, go-karting."

"I know, but Mikey's not interested in any of that now. All he seems to do all day is stare at his phone. I'm glad we didn't have social media when we were kids. It drives me crazy. Just listen to me. I sound like Grandma Grump, don't I?"

"A bit, yeah. What about Lizzie? Is she still sports mad?"

"Absolutely. She's just been made captain of the netball team."

"Good for her. She must take after her auntie."

"Which auntie would that be?"

"Cheek. I was sporty when I was young."

"Don't make me laugh, Jill. You used to hide in the changing rooms to get out of sports."

"Rubbish. I've been meaning to ask you for a while now. Has Lizzie mentioned seeing ghosts recently?"

"No, thank goodness. She seemed to grow out of that phase a couple of years ago. By the way, I've got the tickets for Thursday next week."

"What tickets?"

"For the play."

"What play?"

"The amdram production. Didn't Jack tell you?"

"No, he didn't. I'm pretty sure I would have remembered."

She reached into her handbag. "Here you are."

"Murder at the Ski Lodge? Sounds great."

"It'll do you good to get out of the house."

"I don't suppose it can be any worse than the last play you dragged me to. Can it? Please tell me it can't."

"It'll be good. You'll see."

Suddenly, a man came charging through the door, brandishing what looked like a shotgun.

"Everyone! Get down on the floor!" He slammed the door closed. "Now!"

One look at the gun, and no one needed telling twice.

"What's going on?" Kathy whispered when we were lying under the table.

"Shut up!" he yelled. "Don't make another sound or you'll be sorry!"

He took up a position to one side of the window. Moments later, the sound of sirens could be heard, and three police cars pulled up outside.

Nothing much seemed to happen for the next few minutes. Staff and customers alike were still lying on the floor under the tables, and a few of them were sobbing. The gunman, who was still standing to one side of the window, kept glancing outside at the ever-growing police presence.

The silence was broken by the ringing of the phone behind the counter.

"Shall I get that?" The young shop assistant asked, nervously.

"No, leave it." The man waved the gun in her direction. "Don't move!"

The policeman nearest to the shop picked up a megaphone and began to address the gunman. "You in there, pick up the phone, so we can talk."

The gunman continued to ignore the ringing.

The policeman tried again, "Pick up the phone and we can sort this out without anyone getting hurt."

This time, the gunman shouted to the young woman behind the counter, "You! Pick up the phone."

She got to her feet slowly, and I could see that her hands were shaking. "What should I say?"

"Just pick up the phone." He snapped.

"Hello?" She listened for a few seconds, and then put

her hand over the mouthpiece. "The policeman says it would be better for everyone if you would talk to him."

"Tell him I've got nothing to say to him. Tell him if he doesn't clear the road and get a car for me in the next thirty minutes, I'm going to start shooting people."

She quickly relayed the information to the police.

"They say they'll need more time."

"Tell them they have thirty minutes, then I start shooting!"

She did as she was told.

"Now hang up the phone and get back down on the floor."

Outside, the policeman continued to try to engage the gunman by using the megaphone, but he was having none of it. The phone rang several more times, but the gunman ignored it; he just kept checking his watch.

"I think he means business," Kathy whispered. "He looks crazy enough to do something stupid."

She was right; he did.

I couldn't just lie there and wait for him to start shooting; it was time for me to take control of the situation.

"Jill, what are you doing?" Kathy tried to grab my hand, but I pulled away from her and stood up.

The gunman had his back to me; his attention was focussed on the activity out on the street. When I was within a few feet of him, he must have heard my footsteps because he spun around.

"What do you think you're doing?" He pointed the gun straight at me. "One more step and I'll shoot."

"You don't want to do that."

"I'm warning you."

The words were no sooner out of his mouth than he dropped the gun and fell to the ground, fast asleep. Phew! The 'sleep' spell had done its trick.

I walked over to him and picked up the gun.

The police had obviously seen what had happened because they came charging through the door. One of them took the gun from me; two others grabbed the sleeping man, and carried him out of the shop and into a police van.

"Everyone, can I have your attention, please!" It was the policeman who'd been using the megaphone. "The danger is over now. You can get to your feet."

Everyone did as he said. Some people were in tears, others were hugging one another.

Kathy came running over and threw her arms around me. "What were you thinking, Jill? You could have been killed. Are you okay?"

"I'm fine."

The officer who appeared to be in charge came over to talk to me.

"What exactly happened in here just now, Miss?"

"I don't know. I was trying to talk to him when he seemed to pass out and drop the gun."

"That was a very dangerous thing you did."

"I know. It was stupid. I'm sorry."

The officer called again for everyone's attention. "I realise that you've all just been through a terrible ordeal, but I have to ask you to stick around until my colleagues have taken your names and addresses. Counselling will be available for those who need it."

"What about the shop?" said the woman behind the

counter. "Can I stay open?"

"I'm afraid not. This is now a crime scene. You'll have to close for the time being."

"For how long?"

"I couldn't really say, but we won't keep it closed any longer than is absolutely essential."

After we'd given our details to the police, I walked Kathy down to her shop.

"Are you sure you're okay?" I said.

"I'm fine. You were really brave back there."

"Really stupid, more like."

We were interrupted by the sound of both of our phones ringing. Peter was checking Kathy was alright, and Jack was doing the same thing for me.

"I've been trying to call you ever since I heard the news," he said. "I couldn't get through. I reckon they must have disabled the phone masts so the gunman couldn't contact anyone. Are you okay?"

"Everyone's fine."

"What happened?"

"I'm going to call it a day and come home. I'll tell you everything when I get back."

"Okay, but you're sure you're alright?"

"Positive, honestly. I'll see you soon."

**

My drive home to Middle Tweaking was a longer journey than the one I'd had when we lived in Smallwash, but it was well worth it. We loved the picturesque village and we adored the old watermill.

Six years earlier, when Myrtle Turtle had sold up and moved to the coast, I couldn't have dreamed that one day we would live in that property. Tragedy had struck nine months ago when out of the blue, Jack's dad, Roy, had died of a heart attack. Obviously, it had hit Jack very hard, but he'd soon rallied when his father and mother had both made contact with him. Knowing they'd been reunited in Ghost Town had really lifted Jack's spirits. Pun definitely intended.

Jack's dad had left him a substantial amount of money, including the proceeds from the sale of his house. That money had enabled us to purchase the old watermill which, fortuitously, had just come back onto the market. I still had to pinch myself every morning when I woke up and found myself living there.

Another plus to living in Middle Tweaking was that I no longer had to endure the toll bridge. Even better, I didn't have to put up with Mr Ivers and his ramblings.

I parked in front of the house, and I'd no sooner walked through the gate than the door opened.

"Mummy! Mummy!" My beautiful daughter came running up the path and threw herself into my waiting arms. "I drew a frog at school today."

"Did you, darling? That was very clever of you."

"Would you like to see it?"

"Of course I would."

"It's purple."

"*Purple*? How unusual." I carried her to the door where Jack was waiting for us. "Florence tells me that she drew a frog at school today."

"She certainly did." Jack raised his eyebrows. "Just wait

until you see it."

"Why don't you go and get your picture?" I put her down, and she ran into the house.

"Are you sure you're alright?" Jack said.

"Yes, honestly, but I don't want to talk about it in front of Florence."

"Okay. I'd better go and check on the oven."

"Look, Mummy!" Florence came running back, sheet of paper in hand. "Look at my frog." It was just as well that she'd told me what the drawing was, because it could have been any animal, vegetable or mineral. "Do you like it, Mummy?"

"It's the nicest frog I've ever seen."

"His name is William."

"That's a great name."

"William is one of my friends at school. That's why I called the frog William."

"Did you tell William you'd done that?"

"Yes. He named his elephant Florence."

"That was nice of him. What else did you do at school today?"

"Jackie ripped her skirt when she climbed on the fence. Miss said that we shouldn't climb, so it was her own fault, wasn't it, Mummy?"

"Yes, it was. You have to do what the teacher tells you."

"I was going to mend it for her, but you said I mustn't use magic."

"That's right, I did. You're a good girl for remembering."

"Why can't I, Mummy? I could have mended her skirt and then she would have been happy."

"Don't you remember the talk we had about that,

Florence? Magic has to be our secret because it might frighten other people. We don't want to scare anyone, do we?"

"No, but I wish I could have mended Jackie's skirt. I'm hungry now."

"Me too."

"Daddy has made pancakes!"

"Yummy. Nice one, Daddy."

Chapter 3

It was almost seven-thirty when Jack finally made it back downstairs from taking Florence to bed.

"Did you fall asleep up there?" I said.

"No, she kept asking me to read the story again."

"I thought we'd agreed that we were only going to read it twice each night."

"I know that's what we said, but you know what she's like."

"I know she can wrap you around her little finger. When it's my turn to read her a story, she knows that Mummy is only going to read it twice, and then I'm going downstairs."

"You're right, I know. I'm much too soft with her." He sat on the sofa.

"You don't have time to sit down. The babysitter will be here in fifteen minutes. You do still want to go out, don't you?"

"Definitely, I've been looking forward to it. I'll go and get changed now."

When we'd lived in Smallwash, we'd had a regular babysitter, but it was too far for her to come all this way. I'd asked around, and a couple of people had recommended a young girl called Sarah who was sixteen and lived on the other side of the village. She'd popped in to see us last week, so we could introduce her to Florence. The two of them had hit it off straight away, and both Jack and I liked her.

Jack had just made it downstairs when there was a knock at the door.

"Sarah, come in." I took her coat. "We really appreciate you doing this at short notice."

"No problem. I love babysitting, and the extra money comes in handy."

"You're still at school, aren't you?"

"Yeah, I'm doing my A levels, and I'm hoping to go to nursing college after that." She glanced around. "Is Florence still up?"

"No, her bedtime is at seven. She's probably not asleep yet, but I wouldn't go up there unless she shouts."

"Okay. I've brought some homework with me, so I've got plenty to do."

"There are snacks in the cupboard, and pop in the fridge. Help yourself to anything you like."

"Thank you. Are you two going anywhere nice?"

"We're just nipping down to The Middle."

"We often go there for Sunday lunch; the food is very good. How do you like your new house?"

"We absolutely adore it."

"My mum has always said she wished she could live here. She told me that you're a private investigator."

"That's right. I am."

"That must be really exciting."

"It has its moments." I checked my watch. "We'd better get going. You've got our numbers if you need us, haven't you?"

"Yeah, they're in my phone."

"Okay then, we'll see you later."

"Sarah seems really nice," Jack said, as we walked through the village to the pub.

"She's lovely. I just hope that Florence doesn't decide to

play her up. You know what that little madam can be like. I wouldn't be surprised if she was listening at the bedroom door and shouted to Sarah as soon as we'd left."

The pub was very quiet; there couldn't have been more than a dozen people in there altogether. The middle-aged man behind the bar had a round, ruddy face.

"Good evening. Aren't you the newbies who moved into the old watermill?"

"We are. I'm Jill and this is Jack."

"*Jack and Jill*? You two were clearly made for one another. I'm Arthur Spraggs. What can I get for you to drink?"

"I'll have a medium white wine, please."

"And you, Jack?"

"A glass of your best beer, please."

"White wine and a beer coming up. Will you be eating with us tonight?"

"We most certainly will."

"In that case, why don't you grab a table, and I'll bring your drinks over. You'll find menus on the table."

Ten minutes later, Arthur had brought over the drinks and taken our food order.

"I hear you intentionally put yourself in harm's way today." Jack frowned.

"Who told you?"

"I called one of my old mates at the station, to find out what had happened. He said you walked straight up to the gunman."

"Someone had to do something. The man was clearly deranged, and he'd threatened to start shooting people."

"You should have let the police deal with it."

"By the time they'd got through the door, he could have killed half a dozen people. Anyway, I had magic on my side, so I wasn't really at risk."

"What did you do exactly?"

"I cast the 'sleep' spell on him, and he dozed off and dropped the gun."

"How on Earth did you explain that away to the police?"

"I said that he must have passed out."

"And they believed you?"

"Why wouldn't they? They were hardly going to suspect me of using magic, were they?"

"You scare me sometimes, Jill."

"There's really no need to worry. You should know that by now. What else did your friend tell you about the robbery?"

"Apparently, two men had robbed the bank. The police arrived just as they left the building. One man made a run for the coffee shop, and the other guy got away with the money."

"I only saw the one guy."

"Apparently, they have one of them on CCTV in the bank and leaving the building."

"Only one?"

"Yeah. Your guy. The gunman in the coffee shop."

"What about the other man? How come he wasn't caught on CCTV?"

"I've no idea. He seems to have disappeared into thin air. With all the money."

"I assume the police are still looking for him?"

"Yeah, in Washbridge and the surrounding area, but so

far no luck. What about Kathy? Was she okay?"

"Yeah, she's fine. That reminds me, is there something you forgot to tell me?"

"I don't think so."

"About the ski lodge?"

"*Ski*—? Oh, right, you mean the play."

"The play you signed us up to see without consulting with me."

"It might be good."

"And you're basing that on what, exactly? Have you ever seen a good amdram production?"

"Well, I—err—"

"I rest my case."

Arthur appeared at the table with our food. "There you go, Jill, chicken and chips for you. And scampi and chips for you, Jack. Enjoy."

"This looks nice," Jack said.

"Mmm, it does. I'm ready for this. I'm starving."

"That thing Florence said earlier was a bit worrying, wasn't it?" Jack popped a chip into his mouth.

"About the girl at school who ripped her skirt?"

"Yeah. Florence obviously thought about using magic to repair it."

"But she didn't, and that's what matters. She remembered what we'd told her about having to keep magic a secret."

"This time, yeah, but who knows what will happen next time?"

"There's no point in worrying about it, Jack. We'll just have to cross that bridge if and when we come to it."

"All of this is your grandmother's fault."

"We're not going over that old ground again, are we?"

"But it's true, Jill. You know it is. You and I had decided not to tell Florence that she was a witch until she was older."

"I know what we'd agreed. You don't need to remind me."

"But then, along comes your grandmother, and without a word to you, she unilaterally decides to tell Florence she's a witch. And, as if that wasn't bad enough, she starts to teach her spells."

"You're telling me this as though I don't already know. I'm well aware of what she did. If you recall, she and I fell out over it, and we didn't speak for a couple of months. But what's done is done, and we can't put the clock back. We just have to deal with it, and make sure that Florence keeps her magic under wraps. Now, can we please just enjoy this evening? It's ages since the two of us went out alone."

"Sorry. You're right." He leaned over and gave me a scampi-kiss.

We'd just finished our meal when a man, wearing a flat cap and a sports jacket, came over to our table. For reasons I didn't understand at the time, Jack suddenly started to act nervously.

"Hello again, Jack. How are you?"

"Hi, Stewart. Fine, thanks."

"And this beautiful lady must be your wife."

"Err, yeah, this is Jill. Jill, this is Stewart."

"I'm very pleased to meet you, Jill." He made a show of kissing my hand. "You must be really looking forward to meeting Buddy."

"Who's Buddy?"

"Jack must have told you how cute he is."

I shot Jack a quizzical look.

"Actually, Stewart," Jack piped up. "I haven't got around to telling Jill about Buddy yet."

"Oh? I'm sorry." Stewart stepped back from the table. "I didn't mean to spoil the surprise. I'd best leave you two to it. Give me a call tomorrow, Jack, and we'll sort out the details. It was nice to meet you, Jill."

"Likewise." I waited until he'd moved away and then I turned to Jack. "Is there anything you'd like to tell me, *buddy*?"

"It's a really funny story. You'll laugh when I tell you."

"Try me."

"Okay. I was in the greengrocer's when I happened to spot a notice in the window." He hesitated.

"A notice about?"

"Someone was looking to rehome a dog."

"No! No way."

"Hear me out. While I was looking at the notice, who should walk in but Stewart. And guess what?"

"He bought some turnips?"

"It turned out that he was the one who'd put the notice in the window. How about that for fate?"

"We are not having a dog."

"Don't you think it would be nice for Florence to have a pet?"

"She's too young."

"No, she isn't. I had one at her age. She's always been a little nervous around dogs, having one of her own will help her to get over that fear."

"I'm not sure. What if she's scared of it?"

"It's only a really small dog."

"How small is small?"

"It's a Chihuahua."

"That's not a dog; it's a rat. How come it needs rehoming anyway? What's wrong with him?"

"Nothing. Stewart is going to live in Australia with his brother, and he can't take the dog with him."

"So you agreed to take it?"

"He's such a lovely little thing. I've got a photo. Would you like to see it?"

"No. You do realise that if we take this rat in, he'll be your responsibility, don't you? You're the one who will have to take him for walks and go out in the garden to clean up after him. I'm definitely not going to do it."

"That's okay. I'm at home all day, so it won't be a problem."

Five years ago, Jack had started a website for ten-pin bowling enthusiasts. At the time, it had been no more than a hobby. The website had quickly grown in popularity until the number of regular visitors had become quite significant. At some point, he'd decided to monetize those visitors, and he'd started to sell a range of bowling clothes and accessories. Eventually, he'd decided to take the plunge, give up his job with the police force, and to work on the website full-time.

At the time, I'd been very nervous, but it was what he wanted to do because he'd grown tired of all the politics that went with his job. Fortunately, the gamble had paid off, and now Jack was making almost as much money as he used to earn when he was working full-time. The added bonus was that he could work his own hours from home.

"Have you already told Florence about the dog?" I said.

"No, of course not. I didn't want to do that until you were on board. Look, Jill, if you really are against the idea, I can tell Stewart that we won't be able to take the dog."

"It's okay. You're right. It'll be good for Florence to have something to be responsible for. You'll need to explain to her that she'll have to take the dog for walks with you. And that she'll have to feed him."

"No problem. I think she'll love the idea."

"She will at first, but you know what kids are like. She'll soon get tired of him."

"I'll tell her first thing in the morning."

Arthur came to take away our plates.

"How was the grub, folks?"

"Delicious." Jack nodded his approval.

"Lovely," I agreed. "We'll definitely be dining here again."

"That's good to hear. We have a regular pub quiz on a Wednesday night, and there's an open mic on Fridays. Can either of you sing?"

"Jack can," I said. "He has a great voice."

"No, I don't, Arthur." Jack shot me a look. "Take no notice of her."

"It looks like you two won't be the only newbies in the village soon."

"How come? Is someone else moving in?"

"Haven't you seen the work they're doing on that large property on the left as you come into the village from the north?"

"Yeah, didn't it used to be a hotel or something?"

"That's right. It was the Marples Hotel; it's been empty for five years now. It needed a lot of renovation work."

"It'll make a big house for someone," I said. "Do you know who's bought it?"

"I spoke to the workmen. They didn't know who the buyer was, but they reckon it's going to open as a hotel again. The only thing they could tell me about the new owner is that they're from out of town."

Chapter 4

It seemed silly to drive to the office, only to have to then come all the way back again, so I decided to head straight to Tweaking Manor. I'd been pleased to get out of the house because Jack had made the mistake of telling Florence about the dog. I'd warned him not to say anything before she went to school, but he just couldn't help himself. Of course, once she knew, she wanted to stay home, to be there for Buddy's arrival. When I'd left, Jack was still desperately trying to persuade her that the dog wouldn't come unless she went to school.

It wasn't going well.

Tweaking Manor, which was located approximately halfway between Lower and Middle Tweaking, was best described as a minor stately home. The high wall that surrounded the property was in a terrible state of disrepair: Most of the bricks were flaking, and the iron railings that ran across the top of the wall were rusted, and completely missing in parts. The double gates were open. One of them was hanging off its hinges, and both were rusty and in desperate need of painting.

I drove up the uneven driveway and parked at the side of the property. The house too was showing its age: The brickwork needed pointing, most of the window frames needed replacing, and the guttering had come loose in several sections. The front garden was also in a bad way: The lawn was overgrown, and the flower beds had long since gone to weed.

I rang the doorbell, and moments later, an elderly man with grey hair, dressed in a butler's uniform, answered the door.

"Mrs Maxwell, I presume."

"That's right. You must be Mulgrave."

"Indeed I am, madam. Her ladyship is expecting you."

He led the way into a huge hall, which looked even bigger because it was practically empty. The only furniture was a coat stand to the left of the door, and a badly worn leather sofa against the wall to my right. The walls were all bare except for a cracked mirror above the sofa. Directly in front of me, the double staircase must once have looked magnificent, but was now rather sad and neglected with its threadbare carpet. The room was incredibly cold, and I half expected to be able to see my breath.

"Would you care for a drink, madam?"

"A cup of tea would be nice." If only to warm my hands on.

"Milk and sugar?"

"No sugar and just a drop of milk, please." Life was so much easier since I'd stopped taking sugar. I no longer had to give people lessons in fractions.

"As you wish, madam." He led the way across the wooden floor, which looked as though it hadn't seen a mop in a long time. "This is the dining room; her ladyship is waiting for you in here." He held open the door and I stepped into a room which was much warmer, thanks to the fire that was blazing in the large fireplace.

Caroline, who had a cream-coloured Persian cat on her lap, was seated at the head of a long dining table; she beckoned me to join her.

"Good morning, Jill. This is Olivia."

"Nice to meet you, Olivia." I held out my hand to stroke

the cat, but she hissed at me.

"I'm afraid Olivia is rather anti-social. I must apologise for the state of this old place, I'm afraid our finances aren't in the best shape at the moment, so we've been unable to carry out a lot of the repairs that need to be done."

"It must be very expensive to run a house like this."

"Far too expensive, unfortunately. I can only afford to heat a handful of the rooms. Is Mulgrave getting you a drink?"

"Yes, he's making me a cup of tea. I noticed that he refers to you as your ladyship."

"I've given up trying to stop him. I think he prefers to think he's working for nobility." She smiled. "After you've finished your tea, I'll get him to show you the games room where the goblet was kept."

"Will I be able to see the rest of the house too?"

"If you wish, but a lot of it has been sealed off to reduce costs."

"I hope you don't mind my asking, but is there a 'Lord Tweaking'? Are you married?"

"Rupert died over ten years ago. His ticker."

"Heart attack? I'm sorry."

"No, his heart was fine. Strong as an ox. He died when the grandfather clock fell on top of him. I'd been telling him to get rid of that monstrosity for years, but he was too attached to it to let it go. The silly old goat was trying to move it when it toppled over and crushed him."

"I'm so sorry. That must have been terrible for you."

"Not really. He was an awful man. I should have listened when my parents warned me to stay clear of him. Anyway, back to the matter in hand. After I left your office yesterday, I had something of a brainwave."

"Oh?"

"It occurred to me that my family are scattered to all corners of the land, so it seems silly to ask you to travel up and down the country just to talk to them."

"I don't mind. That's what you're paying me for."

"Precisely. I don't see why I should have to cover that cost when they could just as easily come to Tweaking Manor. I've been in touch with all of them and told them that's what they must do."

"Are they all okay with that?"

"They'll do as I tell them." She grinned. "I've drawn up a list of when each of them will be here." She handed me a sheet of paper. "If this works for you, you'll be able to talk to all of them within the next three to four days."

"I should be able to work with this, thanks. Just one more thing, though, I notice that the cook, Mrs Jones, isn't on this list. Will I be able to speak to her too?"

"Of course, but I thought as she's local, you'd be able to contact her yourself. Is that alright?"

"Absolutely."

After I'd finished my drink, Caroline leaned back in her chair, and pulled on a long cord. Moments later, Mulgrave came back into the room.

"You rang, madam?"

"Would you show Mrs Maxwell to the games room?"

"Certainly, your ladyship. This way, please, Mrs Maxwell."

"Thank you for your time, Caroline." I stood up. "Obviously, I'll be popping in over the next few days to speak to your relatives."

"I'll have Mulgrave prepare one of the reception rooms

for your use. If you need me at any time, I'm usually somewhere around."

The games room was on the opposite side of the house from the dining room, so we walked back through the large entrance hall and down a long corridor.

"Shoo, Harold! You know you shouldn't be in here." Mulgrave pushed the large ginger cat off the billiard table. "The goblet was kept on the shelf over there."

I walked around the billiard table to take a closer look. "Caro—err—Lady Tweaking told me that this room isn't usually locked?"

"That's correct, madam. I'm not sure anyone even knows where the key is."

"And the goblet? Has it always been kept in here?"

"Yes, at least for as long as I've worked here."

"Apart from yourself and Mrs Jones, does Lady Tweaking employ any other domestic staff?"

"No, madam. The family used to, some years ago, but her ladyship had to let them go. Nowadays, she uses an external cleaning company who come in every few weeks, but they only clean certain rooms: The dining room, this room and a couple of the bedrooms. And, of course, the kitchen."

"Is this games room used often?"

"Not really. When his lordship was alive, he used to enjoy a game of billiards. These days, though, it's only used when the family visits."

"As on the night of the birthday dinner?"

"That's right, madam."

"Do you know who was in this room that night?"

"I couldn't say for sure, but I believe Mr Ransom and

Mr Dominic were playing billiards."

"Mr Ransom?"

"Her ladyship's brother. Mr Dominic is her son."

"Did anyone else join them?"

"As I said, I can't be sure, but I don't think so."

I walked over to the two large windows which, judging by the thickness of the paint on the frames, hadn't been opened for a very long time.

"Apart from these windows, I assume the door we came through is the only way in and out of this room?"

"Actually, madam, there is one other way."

"Oh?" I glanced around, but I could see no sign of another door. "Where's that?"

Mulgrave walked over to one corner of the room where a large bookcase was standing. He pulled on one of the books on the top shelf, and the whole bookcase slid to one side, to reveal a rather dimly lit passageway.

"Please follow me, madam. Be very careful because it's quite dark in here, and the floor is rather uneven."

He wasn't kidding. I could barely see my hand in front of me, but I just about managed to follow him along the passageway.

"Are there other secret passageways in the house, Mulgrave?"

"A few, yes, but most of them are sealed off now. This is the only one that's still used regularly."

After we'd been walking for a few minutes, we came to what appeared to be a dead end. I expected him to turn around, but instead, he touched one of the stones, and the wall in front of us slid to one side. To my surprise, I found myself back in the dining room with Caroline.

"I see Mulgrave has shown you the secret passage."

"He tells me this is the only one still in regular use."

"Yes, mainly by the menfolk who like to sneak away for a game of billiards when they think no one will notice."

"What about the other passageways?"

"Sealed off or forgotten."

"Forgotten?"

"So the rumours go. According to legend there are ten secret passageways in this house, but we know of only nine: the one you have just walked through and eight others which have been sealed off."

"And the other one? The tenth?"

"It may or may not even exist. My guess would be that it doesn't."

Mulgrave gave me a tour of the rest of the house, but there wasn't a great deal to see. Most of the rooms were sealed off or empty. It was clear that Caroline now occupied only a small fraction of the house.

"For how long has so much of the building been sealed off, Mulgrave?"

"Only for the last few years. Before that, most of the house was in regular use. Lady Tweaking and his Lordship used to host regular gatherings here. The house was always full of life in those days."

As I drove to Washbridge, I reflected on the sorry state of Tweaking Manor, and I couldn't help but wonder what had led to such a rapid decline in the family's fortunes. I would need to carry out some research into the Tweaking family, to see what I could learn about their current financial problems, and whether that might have any bearing on the disappearance of the goblet.

***

Back at the office building, I could hear sounds coming from down the corridor. Our new neighbours must be in the process of moving in. Whoever they were, it couldn't be any worse than having a clown school on your doorstep.

More famous last words.

"Good morning, Mrs V."

"Morning, Jill."

"Any messages?"

"None so far. It's been very quiet, but I have found out the name of the business that's moving in down the corridor. It's called Bubbles."

"How do you know?"

"I saw two men carrying the sign upstairs."

"Bubbles? I suppose it could be one of those places that sell fancy soap."

"Surely they would need a shopfront."

"You're right. What else could Bubbles be, I wonder?"

"I've no idea. Intriguing, isn't it, Jill?"

"Very. Keep your eyes peeled and let me know when you find out more."

When I walked through to my office, Winky was deep in conversation with another cat. Neither of them appeared to have noticed me, so I went online to search for more information on the Tweaking family. The most recent articles were from six months earlier, and related to a long-standing dispute with HMRC, regarding alleged unpaid taxes. The matter, which had dragged on for a number of years, had finally been decided in favour of HMRC, leaving the Tweaking family, and Caroline in particular, with an enormous tax bill. That explained the dire state of her finances. The article went on to suggest that the family might have to sell Tweaking Manor in order to pay off their debts.

Twenty minutes later, after Winky and his visitor had finished their business, the other cat made his exit through the window.

"What was that all about, Winky?"

"That's Carl the Coach."

"What did he want?"

"He's my life coach."

"*You* have a life coach? Since when?"

"I've been with him for a couple of months now."

"And how's it going?"

"Fantastically well. Anyway, I can't hang around here, chatting all day. Places to meet, people to go. Later."

And with that, he too disappeared out of the window.

Chapter 5

I was still thinking about Winky and his life coach when Mrs V popped her head around the door.

"Jill, Mr Edwards is here to see you."

"Mr Edwards?"

She walked in and closed the door behind her.

"Don't you remember? I told you last Friday that he'd made an appointment for today. Didn't you put it in your diary?"

I took my diary from the drawer and opened it at today's page. It was blank.

"Err, Mr Edwards. Yes, I have him down here." Mrs V tried to sneak a look, but I was too quick for her, and snapped the diary closed. "Send him in, please."

Mr Edwards was eighty-two, but he certainly didn't dress like an octogenarian. He was wearing trainers, jeans and a bomber jacket, and looked as though he'd just come from an audition for Grease.

"Mr Edwards, do have a seat."

"Please call me Rusty. Everyone does, on account of my hair." He ran his fingers through what was left of his white hair.

"Right? Okay, Rusty it is, and I'm Jill. What can I do for you today?"

"I want you to prove to everyone that I haven't lost my marbles."

Judging by what I'd seen and heard so far, that might be a tall order.

"That's quite an unusual request, Rusty. Could you perhaps elaborate a little?"

"Certainly. It all started last Wednesday. I was in my reading room, which is at the rear of the house. I go there whenever I'm in the mood for a cigar. The late Mrs Edwards didn't approve of my smoking, so she banished me to the reading room. Even though I lost poor Edith a couple of years ago, I still go in there to smoke." He chuckled. "Just in case her ghost is watching me. Anyway, I was in the reading room, looking through my binoculars when—"

"Sorry to interrupt, Rusty, but did you just say *binoculars*?"

"That's right. My property backs onto Wash Green Park. Do you know it?"

"I don't think so."

"It's only a small park. I like to look at the wildlife, particularly the squirrels. I do love a good squirrel, don't you?"

"Err, yeah. I guess."

"I was watching one particular squirrel, as it ran up the side of a tree, when I noticed movement in one of the properties on the opposite side of the park. A man and a woman were standing next to the window. I didn't think anything of it at the time, and I was just about to look away when I saw her shoot him."

"She shot him? Are you sure?"

"Absolutely. She held out a gun and let him have it. The poor guy didn't stand a chance."

"What did you do?"

"Called the police of course, but they didn't take me seriously at first."

"Why ever not? You'd just witnessed a shooting. Possibly a murder."

"I've had a few issues previously with the local police."

"What kind of issues?"

"There was the incident with the roundabout."

"Roundabout?"

"Some kids were pushing it in an anti-clockwise direction."

"I see. Err, actually, no I don't see. What's wrong with that?"

"Everyone knows that roundabouts should turn clockwise."

"Right. Any other incidents?"

"There were the pigeons."

"What about them?"

"They were taking bread that was clearly intended for the ducks."

"And you contacted the police about that?"

"Naturally."

"When you contacted them about the shooting, what happened?"

"They did eventually send someone, but the officer who called to see me seemed more interested in why I was using binoculars to look into other people's houses. I told him about the squirrels, but I'm not sure he believed me. Anyway, to cut a long story short, he did eventually go over to the property."

"What did he find?"

"According to the policeman, the couple who live there were both alive and well, and they denied any knowledge of the incident that I'd witnessed."

"What happened next?"

"Nothing. As far as the police were concerned, no crime had been committed, so that was an end to it. That was bad enough, but they as good as insinuated that I was a sandwich short of a — err — "

"Picnic?"

"I couldn't just now, thanks. I have a lot on today."

"No, I meant — never mind. You were saying that the police had made certain insinuations?"

"Yes. That I was a crazy old man, and even some kind of Peeping Tom, spying on my neighbours."

"That's awful."

"It certainly is. I will not simply stand by and allow my reputation to be besmirched in that way, which is where you come in, young lady."

"What exactly is it you want from me?"

"The only way to clear my name is to prove that I did in fact see what I reported."

"The shooting?"

"Correct. Are you up for the challenge?"

"Sure, but I'm going to need a lot more information from you."

"Of course. Why don't we continue this discussion at my place? That way I can show you my reading room and point out the property in question."

"That sounds like a plan. I could pop over tomorrow, or is that too soon?"

"Tomorrow works for me." He stood up. "Give me a call about an hour before you intend to come over and I'll put the kettle on."

He'd no sooner left the office than Winky jumped onto my desk.

"Rusty is quite a character, isn't he?" I said.

"Hmm. *Character* is one word for him. Nutjob is a better

one."

"What do you mean? He seems harmless enough."

"You surely didn't buy into that story of his, did you? Using the binoculars to look at squirrels? The man is clearly a Peeping Tom."

"That's a bit rich coming from you," I scoffed. "It's not that long ago that you had a telescope in here."

"That was totally different. I was stargazing, as well you know."

"That's not how I remember it."

I heard voices in the outer office, so being the curious (okay, nosy) person I am, I went to see who it was. Mrs V was in conversation with a woman of about the same age.

"Maud, this is my boss, Jill Maxwell."

"I'm very pleased to make your acquaintance, Mrs Maxwell." She held out her gloved hand. "I'm Mrs Mizus."

"Mrs Mrs?"

"That's right."

"Sorry, I must have misheard. Mrs — ?"

"Mizus."

I was still puzzled, and it must have shown because Mrs V came to my rescue. "Maud Mizus. M-I-Z-U-S."

"Oh, Mrs *Mizus*. I thought you said Mrs Mrs. Like, Mrs squared." I laughed. "I imagine you get that a lot."

"No." Mrs Mizus said, stony-faced. "This is the first time."

"Right. Just me, then."

"Maud is something of an internet star," Mrs V said.

"I wouldn't go that far, Annabel." Mrs Mizus waved away the idea.

"It's true. She has over one thousand followers, Jill."

"Right." I did my best to sound suitably impressed. "That's — err — fantastic."

"I wondered if I might give it a try," Mrs V said. "Going online, I mean. But Maud says it's probably too complicated for me."

"You never have been very technically minded, have you, Annabel?" Maud said.

"Not really. It takes me all my time to use the TV remote."

***

Later that same afternoon, I had a surprise visitor.

I hadn't seen Mad for almost three years, since she'd relocated to the Glasgow office.

"You're looking great, Mad. Grab a seat, and I'll get Mrs V to make us a drink."

"Don't bother with the drink. I can't stay for more than a few minutes. I only popped in to let you know that I'm back."

"Just visiting, I assume?"

"No, I'm back to stay. Actually, I've been here for almost a month, but I've been so busy that I've not had the chance to get in touch."

"Are you still doing the ghost hunting?"

"What else would I do?"

"How come you're back here?"

"Good question. I thought I'd finally seen the back of Washbridge, but then I got a call from the powers-that-be, so here I am again. Like a bad penny."

"Don't be daft. I for one am glad you're back. This place

wasn't the same without you."

"That's nice of you to say. I'm sorry I haven't kept in touch as often as I should have, but I was really busy up in Scotland."

"Don't give it a second thought. I know what it's like to be busy, trust me. Anyway, you're here now, so you can update me on all your news."

"There's not much to report, really." She grinned and held out her left hand.

"You're married?"

"Yep. Two months ago."

"You dark horse. How come I didn't get an invitation to the wedding?"

"No one did. Brad, that's my husband, and I both decided we didn't want a big affair. For obvious reasons, I didn't want my family there, and Brad doesn't have any family to speak of. We booked a date at the local register office, grabbed a couple of witnesses off the street, and Bob's your uncle."

I resisted the urge to make my usual observations vis-à-vis the whole *Uncle Bob* thing.

"That's great. Where are you living now?"

"We have an apartment over by the river. You'll have to come and see it some time."

"I'd love to. Does Brad know that you're a ghost hunter?"

"Yeah, I told him about six months ago."

"Won't that land you in trouble? Telling him, I mean."

"Not really. Luckily, I don't have to worry about rogue retrievers. And anyway, Brad knows he can't tell a soul."

"He must have been a bit freaked out when you told him, wasn't he?"

"At first, yeah. He thought I was drunk, but I managed to convince him in the end, and he seems to have got used to the idea now."

"What does he do for a job?"

"He had his own record shop in Glasgow. When I received my orders to move back down here, I didn't want to leave, and I was going to hand in my notice, but then Brad said he fancied a change of scenery. The next thing I knew, he'd sold his premises in Glasgow, bought a shop in Washbridge, and moved all his stock down here."

"Where is his new shop?"

"Just off the marketplace. It's called Vinyl Alley."

"I thought record shops had had their day. Isn't it all about streaming nowadays?"

"That's true, but Brad focuses solely on vinyl records, and there's been a resurgence in their popularity. The new shop has been open for a couple of weeks now. I'm working in there with him."

"You? Your taste in music was always awful."

"That from the woman who thought the Hoopla Chant was the best song of the decade."

"I was six."

"My new job is a great cover. Much better than when I used to work in the tax office and the library. Anyway, enough about me. How's little Florence doing?"

"She's great, but she can be a bit of a handful."

"I've been meaning to ask; does she know she's a witch?"

"Yes. I hadn't planned to tell her until she was older, but my grandmother had other ideas."

"She told her?"

"Yeah."

"What did you do when you found out?"

"I completely lost it. Grandma and I weren't on speaking terms for ages afterwards."

"Have you made up now?"

"Let's just say there's an uneasy truce between us, but I've warned her that she mustn't teach Florence any more spells."

"Has it caused any problems? Florence knowing she's a witch, I mean?"

"Not up to now, touch wood. But you know what kids are like, and how excitable they can get. Every day she goes to school, I half expect to get a phone call to say she's made the school guinea pig disappear."

"Oh dear." Mad chuckled. "Sorry, I shouldn't laugh. It must be nerve-racking for you." She checked her watch. "I have to get going. Drop into the shop and see us when you get the chance."

"I will, yeah."

***

When I arrived home, Florence came rushing to the door to greet me.

"Mummy, Mummy! Buddy's here. Come and see."

I'd totally forgotten about the stupid Chihuahua, but I didn't want Florence to see my negative reaction, so I managed to conjure up a smile from somewhere.

"I can't wait to meet him, darling."

She took my hand and led me through to the lounge where Jack was on the sofa, with the small dog on his lap.

"Isn't he cute, Mummy?" Florence gushed.

"Err, yeah, he's very nice." For an oversize rat.

"I know you've only just walked through the door," Jack said. "But I had a phone call from Florence's friend, Anne — well, from her mother, to be precise — she asked if Florence could go over there for tea."

"Now?"

"Please, Mummy." Florence pleaded. "Anne has got the super sparkly hairband maker, and she said she would make one for me."

"Wouldn't you rather stay here with Buddy?"

"He can come with me."

"No, he can't. Anne's mummy won't be happy if you show up with a dog." I turned to Jack. "What's with the short notice?"

"Anne was supposed to ask Florence at school yesterday, but she forgot all about it, so now Anne is rather upset. Her mum rang on the off chance that Florence would still be able to go over. I knew you were on your way home from work, so I said it'd be okay."

"Are you sure you want to go, Florence?" I said. "Even if you can't take Buddy?"

"Yes. I want a sparkly hairband."

"Okay, then. You'd better say goodbye to Buddy."

"Bye, Buddy. See you later." She gave the dog a stroke, and then Jack handed the Chihuahua to me.

No sooner were Jack and Florence out of the house than Buddy began to snarl. "Put me down, can't you? I'm fed up with people manhandling me."

"Okay, sorry." I put him on the floor.

"People think that just because I'm small, they have the right to pick me up willy-nilly. Well, they don't!"

"Hey, young man, I think you'd better check your

attitude. You do realise that we've just adopted you, don't you?"

"Is that right? I don't recall anyone consulting me on the matter."

"Would you rather be out on the streets?"

"A pedigree of my standing? I could have my choice of homes. You should consider yourself very lucky to have me."

"You'd better not give Florence any of this attitude, young man."

"Is that the little squirt?"

"Yes, no! You can't call her a little squirt. She's my daughter."

"Whatever."

"Have you been talking to Florence too?"

"I tried, but she blanked me."

"Florence is only young. She hasn't developed all her magical powers yet."

"And as for that other one—" Buddy gave a big sigh.

"You mean Jack?"

"Whatever his name is. What was that slop he gave me to eat earlier?"

"I don't know. I wasn't here."

"It isn't acceptable. I have very exacting requirements when it comes to nutrition."

"You do?"

"Yes. Why don't you get a notepad and I'll tell you what I need?"

Like an idiot, I did as he said. After he'd dictated his list of approved foods, he curled up and was soon fast asleep.

"Isn't he a little beauty?" Jack whispered when he got

back. "He and I are going to be great *buddies*." He laughed. "Buddies? Get it?"

"Hilarious. You'll be pleased to know that Buddy speaks very highly of you too."

"Really?"

"No."

Chapter 6

The next morning, I slept in a little later than usual. By the time I'd showered, dressed, and made my way downstairs, Jack was halfway through his customary bowl of muesli.

"Where's Florence?"

"In the back garden with Buddy."

Shortly before we'd moved into the old watermill, we'd had a fence erected to enclose the back garden. We wanted to ensure Florence couldn't get anywhere near the river that ran by the property. The only access now was through a gate, which was always kept padlocked.

Out in the garden, Florence was throwing a ball for the dog to fetch. Buddy looked on impassively and made no attempt whatsoever to retrieve it. Undeterred, Florence kept on throwing and retrieving the ball herself.

"It doesn't look like Buddy's very excited about playing ball," I said.

"He couldn't be any less interested if he tried." Jack laughed. "I told her it might take a while to train him."

"I'll go outside and have a word with her." I slipped on some shoes and went out into the garden. "Morning, petal."

"Mummy!" She came running over and gave me a hug and a big kiss. "I'm trying to play ball with Buddy, but he won't fetch it."

"Maybe no one has showed him how to do it."

"Will *you* show him, Mummy?"

"I can give it a try. Have you had your orange juice this morning?"

"No, not yet."

"If you go inside and have your juice, I'll see if I can teach Buddy how to fetch the ball."

"Okay." She ran into the house.

Even before I'd had the chance to speak to him, the dog said, "Forget it. If you think I'm chasing around this muddy garden after that stupid ball, you've got another think coming."

"And a very good morning to you too, Buddy."

"I mean it. I'm not chasing after a stupid ball."

"Fair enough, but here's the deal. We'll buy your ridiculously expensive food, but only if you play ball with Florence."

"But it's a stupid game. She throws the ball, I bring it back to her, and then she does the same thing all over again. What's the point of that? I'm not doing it."

"It looks like you're stuck with the 'slop', then."

"That sounds a lot like blackmail."

"Blackmail's a very emotive word. I'd prefer to call it quid pro quo."

"Okay, okay. I'll fetch the ball, but I'm not doing it all day long. Fifteen minutes at a stretch, max."

"That'll do. Do we have a deal?"

"I suppose so, but I want it noted that I'm only agreeing under duress."

"So noted." I went back into the house. "Florence, darling. Buddy knows how to play ball now."

"You're so clever, Mummy."

"That's very true. Why don't you go and play with him again?"

She put on her shoes, ran back out to the garden, and threw the ball for the dog. Buddy didn't exactly sprint after it, but he did manage to pick it up in his mouth and return it to Florence. She was clearly delighted, beaming from ear to ear.

"How on Earth did you manage that?" Jack said.

"All it took was a little negotiation."

"Huh?"

"It seems our friend, Buddy, isn't very impressed by the food you've been giving him."

"What's wrong with it?"

"According to him, it's 'slop'. I promised we'd buy the food he prefers, and in return he's agreed to play ball with Florence."

"Is Florence able to talk to him?"

"No, it'll be a while before her powers have developed enough to allow her to talk to animals. It's probably just as well because I wouldn't want her to hear some of the things Buddy has to say. I'm starving. I'm going to make myself some toast. Do you want any?"

"You'll be lucky. We don't have any bread."

"How come?"

"I called at the local shop yesterday afternoon, but they were all out. That shop's useless, Jill. You can't rely on them to have anything. We're going to have to get all our shopping from the supermarket."

"They must have had a delivery of bread by now. I'll nip over there."

"Okay, but don't say I didn't warn you."

Although we'd lived in Middle Tweaking for a few months, I'd not yet stepped foot in the local shop. The bulk of our shopping was delivered by the closest supermarket. As Jack was home all day, he was able to nip out to pick up anything we ran out of. I was quite sure the local shop couldn't be as bad as Jack had made it out to be — like every man in the world, he had a tendency to exaggerate.

As I made my way across the village, I reflected on how nice it would be to have a 'normal' local shop and shopkeeper, instead of the crazy that had been Little Jack's Corner Shop. Nice as he was, Little Jack was a true eccentric. How else did you explain a man who spent all of his time on stilts in a wind tunnel? During the time we'd lived in Smallwash, he'd tried to introduce all manner of new schemes including loyalty cards, home delivery and online ordering — all of which had failed spectacularly.

Middle Tweaking's village shop, which was next-door to the greengrocer, was called Tweaking Stores. From the outside, it looked slightly smaller than Little Jack's Corner Shop. A bell chimed as I walked through the door, but there didn't appear to be anyone behind the counter. The interior of the shop was quite old fashioned and reminded me of the local shop where I used to buy sweets as a kid. The layout was very confusing because there didn't appear to be any obvious grouping of like items. Instead, everything seemed to have been placed on the shelves in a random fashion.

"Good morning." The woman, who had appeared behind the counter, was wearing a floral-patterned apron and had a blue rinse. "I'm Cynthia Stock. My sister, Marjorie and I own this fine establishment. Are you visiting the village?"

"Actually no. My husband, myself and our little girl moved into the old watermill recently."

"You must be Jack's wife."

"That's right. I'm Jill."

"Your husband has been in here a few times, but I think it's the first time you and I have met, isn't it?"

"Yes, I haven't had the chance to pop in before."

"That little girl of yours is a darling."

"Florence? We like to think so."

"Did you find what you were looking for?"

"Actually no. We found ourselves without bread and butter this morning, and I really fancy toast for breakfast."

"Oh dear." She frowned. "I'm afraid you're out of luck. The bread delivery won't arrive until eleven."

"Isn't that rather late?"

"Actually, it's earlier than usual. It doesn't normally arrive until midday."

"O—kay. What about butter? Where would I find that?"

"Hmm." Her frown deepened. "I'm afraid we're all out of that too. We should be getting some more in tomorrow."

"*Tomorrow?*"

"Or the day after. Definitely by the weekend."

"Right. Okay, well never mind."

"I tell you what we do have, though."

"Yes?" I assumed she was going to offer a non-dairy spread.

I was wrong.

"Yesterday, we took delivery of some lovely body warmers." She pointed to a rack in the corner of the shop. "They're gorgeous and they're very reasonably priced."

"Just in time for spring, presumably?"

"Can I interest you in one?"

"Not just at the moment, thanks. I really had my heart set on bread and butter."

"I'm sorry to have let you down on your first visit to the shop. I'm sure you'll have better luck next time."

Jack had finished his breakfast but was still sitting at the kitchen table. When he saw I'd returned emptyhanded, he grinned. "Still having toast?"

I ignored the jibe, went over to the cupboard, took out the cornflakes and poured some into a bowl.

"I did warn you, Jill."

"I don't understand it. How can they be out of bread *and* butter?"

"Did you meet the sisters Stock?"

"One of them. Stock? Now there's an ironic name if ever there was one. Cynthia tried to sell me a body warmer."

"It's almost May."

"I know. And the layout of that shop makes no sense; there's stuff everywhere. I used to think Little Jack's shop was bad, but at least he stocked the essentials, and the layout made some kind of sense." Out in the garden, Florence was still throwing the ball for Buddy who looked as though he was about to collapse. "It looks like Florence has run him ragged."

***

I'd decided to go directly from the old watermill to Mr Edwards' house. I wanted to see the reading room from which he claimed he'd witnessed a shooting in one of the properties across the park.

There was no off-street parking at the front of the property, but I managed to park on the road just a few doors down. The houses were all clearly expensive, and large enough to accommodate a sizable family, but I was pretty sure that Mr Edwards lived there alone.

"Jill, good morning." He greeted me at the door. "I've just put the kettle on. Is tea okay or would you prefer coffee?"

"Tea would be lovely. Milk no sugar, please."

"I was about to make myself some toast. I don't suppose you'd care for some, would you?"

"Actually, Mr Edwards—"

"Rusty! You really must call me Rusty."

"Sorry. Actually, Rusty, a slice of toast would go down very nicely. I was going to have some before I left home, but we were out of bread and butter, and the local shop didn't have either."

"What?" He looked horrified. "What kind of retail establishment is that? If that were my local shop, I'd be reading the Riot Act to them. Come on in, and I'll get the toast started."

I had to give Rusty his due: the man certainly knew how to make toast. While we ate, we chatted at the kitchen table, mainly about his ex-wife who he clearly still missed.

When we'd finished our tea and toast, he led the way upstairs to the reading room, which was at the rear of the property. Just as he'd described, it overlooked a small park.

"You have a lovely view from up here, Rusty."

"I'm a lucky man. I find it very relaxing to look out over the park, particularly in the spring and summer when I can open the French doors and sit on the balcony."

"Was it through this window that you witnessed the incident in question?"

"Yes. Do you see the house over there? The one with the garage with the red back door?"

"I see it."

"That's the property where the incident took place. In the window on the first floor, to the right."

I can see the window, but I can't see inside the room from here."

"You'll need the binoculars. Let me get them for you." He walked across the room, retrieved what was clearly an expensive pair of binoculars, and handed them to me.

"They're quite heavy," I said.

"They're vintage. None of that new-fangled plastic rubbish. Give them a go."

I did as he said. The lenses were very powerful, and I could now see clearly into the rooms of the properties opposite.

"Tell me, Rusty, how often do you study the park?"

"Most days. As I mentioned when I came to see you, I'm primarily interested in the wildlife. I have some photos that I think you'll find interesting."

"I—err—" For a horrible moment, I had a flashback to what Winky had said about Rusty being a Peeping Tom.

I needn't have worried because all the photos were of squirrels: Squirrels foraging amongst the leaves for nuts, squirrels running up the side of trees, squirrels sitting on benches, and even a few brave ones, going up to passersby and begging for food.

"You're clearly fond of squirrels, Rusty."

"Indeed I am. Such lovely creatures, don't you think?"

"I guess."

Rusty opened a small wooden case and took out the longest cigar I'd ever seen. "Do you like cigars, Jill?"

"I don't smoke."

"What about one for your hubby?"

"He doesn't smoke either."

I gave an involuntary shiver because the temperature in the room had suddenly plummeted.

"Sorry about the cold, Jill. The heating has been on the blink for some time now. I've had the man out a couple of times to check the boiler, but he couldn't find anything wrong with it. The weird thing is that it only ever seems to happen in this room."

"That is weird."

Actually, it wasn't all that weird because, standing in the corner of the room was the ghost of a woman. She walked over and whispered in my ear. "Tell him to throw away those awful things before they kill him, would you?"

"Edith?"

Rusty dropped the cigar. "What did you just say?"

"I said — err — Swedish."

"Swedish?"

"Yes. I heard that Swedish squirrels are the biggest."

"I didn't know that. You live and learn."

Chapter 7

Mrs V was hard at work behind her desk, knitting what looked like a poncho. She had a plaster on her forehead.

"What happened to your head?"

"It was those pesky squirrels, Jill. I always used to think they were such cute little creatures, but I was wrong. They're vicious."

"Are you telling me that a squirrel attacked you?"

"Not attacked, exactly. I was out in the garden, tending to my petunias, when one of the little blighters threw an acorn at me. It almost knocked me out."

"Are you sure it threw it at you? Might the acorn simply have fallen from the tree?"

"I'm positive. It wouldn't have hit me with such force. And, when I looked up, I saw him standing on the branch; he was practically laughing at me."

"Did you have to go to hospital to get it seen to?"

"No, it wasn't that bad. Just a small cut and a bruise. It'll be gone in a day or so."

"What about Armi? Did he get hit with acorns too?"

"Don't mention that man to me."

"What did he do?"

"He was in the house at the time of the acorn incident, watching Cuckoo Corner on the Cuckoo Channel. When I told him what had happened, he laughed."

"That doesn't sound like Armi."

"He did apologise but that was too little too late. I've told him he can make his own dinner for the rest of the week."

"Serves him right. Were there any messages this morning while I was out?"

"No, but you did ask me to remind you that your new accountant is coming in today." Mrs V checked her watch. "In fact, she should be here any time now."

"Oh yes." I sighed. "I'd forgotten about her."

I loathed spending time with accountants. Luther Stone had been the exception, but only because he was good company (and smoking hot). Unfortunately, a few months earlier, Luther had decided to go and live in France. Before he left, he'd passed on all his existing clients to someone who he'd described as one of the superstars of the new wave of accountancy.

Whatever that meant.

"Just remind me, Mrs V, what's my new accountant's name?"

"Rosemond Starr."

"She sounds more like a reality TV personality than an accountant."

"You said you were going to get all your paperwork in order ahead of her visit. Did you remember to do that?"

"Err, yes, of course."

No.

I'd forgotten all about the accountant's visit, so all the bills, receipts, invoices and stuff were in a pile in the bottom drawer of my desk. It was too late to sort them out now, so she'd just have to work with them as they were.

When I walked through to my office, I had the shock of my life.

Winky had eyes. Two of them!

I was so stunned that I took a few steps backwards and almost fell over.

"What do you think of it?" he said.

It took a while, but I eventually managed to compose myself, and took a closer look at him. "Is that an eye patch you're wearing?"

"It certainly is. I was just thinking to myself the other day that it was ages since I'd worn one, so I bought this little number at the weekend. What do you think?"

"It has an eye printed on it."

"I know. Clever, isn't it?"

"No, it's really creepy. Take it off at once."

"I will not. I think it's brilliant. From a distance, people think I have two eyes again."

"It's freaking me out."

"Tough. You'll just have to get used to it."

Ten minutes later, right on the dot, my new accountant arrived. Rosemond Starr, who looked to be in her mid to late twenties, was wearing what could best be described as a power suit, and she had the haircut to match.

After strutting confidently into the room, she proceeded to crush my hand with her 'power' handshake.

"You must be Jill. I'm very pleased to meet you."

"Likewise, Rosemond."

"Please call me Starr. Everyone does."

"Okay, err—Starr."

"I trust that Luther Stone told you something about my background."

"He said you came highly recommended. And something about you being the new wave of accountancy?"

"Quite. The thing is, Jill, the era of the old-style accountant has gone, as I'm sure you'll agree."

"Err, I—err—"

"Long gone are the days when an accountant could simply juggle figures and balance the books. These days, the modern-day accountant is far more than a number cruncher. It's our responsibility to help drive our client's business forward. It's all about blue sky thinking, don't you agree?"

"Blue sky — err — "

"And, of course, thinking outside the box."

"Right."

"It's my mission to maximise the potential of your business based on the synergy of my business acumen and your skills as a — err — what is it you do again?"

"I'm a private investigator."

"Right. Once we've harnessed our combined skillsets, you can expect to see your business grow exponentially. What do you say?"

I was getting a migraine just listening to her. "That all sounds — err — great."

"Excellent." She took a file from her briefcase. "Looking through Luther's notes, I see that you don't have any kind of management reporting system in place. We'll have to remedy that."

"Will we?"

"You need reports that tell you which of the jobs you're working on are profitable. That will help you to keep a tight grip on your cashflow, and to monitor your performance against budget. All the useful stuff that I'm sure you've been dying to have."

"I — err — "

"I suppose we'd better make a start by going through your income and expenditure for the last couple of months. Have you prepared that for me as I requested?"

"Actually, I—err—" I pulled open the bottom drawer, and glanced at the pile of receipts, invoices and goodness knows what else. "Err, yes, I have."

"Excellent."

"Unfortunately, I left it all at home." I pushed the drawer closed.

"Oh?"

"I'm really sorry, but I was called out on an urgent case first thing this morning, and I totally forgot to pick up the paperwork I'd prepared for you."

"Never mind. I suppose I could pop in again next month, and we'll catch up on it all then."

"Great."

"This does tie in rather nicely to something else I wanted to discuss with you today. Recording your income and expenditure by collecting dozens of scraps of paper is now totally outdated."

"It is?"

"Absolutely. That system belongs back in the dark ages. Do you have a mobile phone, Jill?"

"Yes."

"Excellent. Could I borrow it?"

"Err, sure." I handed it to her.

"I'm just going to install an app called SnapExp."

"Is that some kind of dating app?"

"No." She laughed. "Every time you get a bill or receipt, use this app to scan it. The app will automatically input the details into the accounting system, which means that your accounts will be up to date all of the time. It also means when we have these meetings, we'll be able to have much more meaningful discussions about your business, rather than having to sift through mountains of paperwork. Does that work for you?"

"I guess so. Is it difficult to use?"

"Not at all. You simply use it as you would a camera. Put the receipt or invoice on the desk, snap a picture of it with the app, and Bob's your uncle."

How many more times? No, he isn't.

"So?" Mrs V said, after Starr had left. "What did you make of your new accountant?"

"To be perfectly honest, I didn't really take to her. She's too much. Much too much. I just need somebody who will sort out my books and tell me how much money I've made."

"Or lost."

"Thanks for that, Mrs V. That Starr woman wants to take over my business. She was talking about blue sky boxes—whatever they are. And she's put this stupid app on my phone."

"What does it do?"

"I'm supposed to take pictures of all my bills and receipts, but I don't really have a clue how to use it."

"What are you going to do about her?"

"I'm not sure. Look for another accountant probably. An old-school one who just wants to deal with numbers."

Mrs V was just about to leave my office when she glanced over at Winky and almost jumped out of her skin.

"Why would you buy him that horrible eye patch, Jill? It looks like his eye has grown back."

"I didn't buy it."

"Who did, then?"

"I—err—I'm going to get rid of it."

"Please do. It's making me feel queasy."

After she'd left the office. I turned to Winky. "See? What did I tell you? Nobody likes your new eye patch."

"I don't care what anyone else thinks, and what do you mean, you're going to get rid of it? I'd like to see you try."

***

I'd decided to call it a day, and I was just about to go downstairs, when I saw a woman come out of the door at the other end of the corridor. I thought I should go over and introduce myself.

"Hi, there. I'm Jill Maxwell. I work in the office just down the corridor."

"I'm Farah. Farah Close. You must be the private investigator."

"That's me." I glanced up at the sign. "Bubbles? We were trying to work out what kind of business it might be. Are you a hairdresser?"

"Actually, no. I'm a dog groomer. I've been working as a mobile groomer until now. This is the first place I've had of my own. I'm really very excited. Do you have dogs, Jill?"

"Yes, one. Well, two, I suppose." She gave me a puzzled look. "It's a little complicated. I have a Chihuahua at home."

"Such lovely dogs, and very easy to groom too."

"My 'other' dog doesn't actually live with me all the time. He's a Labradoodle."

"That's a very different proposition. They're very lively dogs, as I'm sure you know. Much more expensive when it comes to the grooming. We open next Monday; all shampoos will be free on that day, on a first-come, first-served basis."

"Well, the very best of luck with your new venture."

"Thanks, Jill. Drop by for a cup of tea any time you like."

***

I'd intended to pop into one of the shops in Washbridge city centre, to pick up some custard creams because I'd eaten the last one that morning. Unfortunately, I'd been so busy with the new accountant, and so distracted by Winky's freaky eye patch, that it had totally slipped my mind. Not a problem. The local store in Middle Tweaking was bound to stock the most popular biscuits in the country.

I parked outside the old watermill, but instead of going straight into the house, I nipped over to the store. Once inside, it quickly became obvious that the main problem would be locating the biscuits. They could literally be anywhere. I did find some ginger nuts, which were next to the cabbages. On a separate aisle, I found fig biscuits, Garibaldis, and Jammie Dodgers, next to the breakfast cereal. But, as for custard creams, I drew a complete blank.

Behind the counter, Cynthia Stock was writing in what looked like a large, old fashioned ledger.

"Hello, Jill. Sorry, I didn't notice you come in. I'm just updating my stock book."

"Is that really where you record your stock?"

"Yes, we've used books like this one for years. It's a foolproof method. Every now and then, we get someone in here, trying to sell us one of those new-fangled computer systems, but you can't beat pen and paper, can you?"

"Err, I guess not."

I'd always thought I was something of a Luddite, but compared to Mrs Stock, I was at the cutting edge of technology. "I just popped in for some custard creams. Do you know where I could find them?"

"Did you check next to the tea bags, Jill?"

"No, I didn't. Where are the tea bags?"

"Next to the carrots. If you turn around, it's the third aisle from the left."

"Okay. I'll take a look."

I followed her directions and found the carrots and the tea bags, but there was no sign of the custard creams—just an ominous gap where they should have been.

Back at the counter, I told Mrs Stock that there were no custard creams on the shelf.

"Oh dear." She began to flick through her ledger. "Let me see. Custard creams? Here they are. According to this, we were down to our last packet on Monday. That should have triggered a new order, but Marjorie seems to have missed it."

"Marjorie's your sister, isn't she?"

"That's right. I'll have a word with her later about this. It really isn't good enough."

"I wouldn't want to cause any trouble."

"How about a packet of Garibaldis? Or Jammie Dodgers? And there are always ginger nuts."

"No, thanks. I had my heart set on custard creams."

"I'll order some straight away."

"Thanks. When are you likely to receive them?"

"Next week, hopefully. The week after at the very latest."

Somewhat disgruntled at the prospect of an evening sans custard creams, I made my way back to the old watermill. I expected Florence to meet me at the gate, but there was no sign of her. She didn't even appear when I stepped into the house.

Jack was all alone in the kitchen.

"Where's Florence?"

He gestured towards the window. "Out in the garden, playing ball with Buddy."

"How long have they been out there?"

"Ever since she got back from school. That poor little dog will definitely sleep well tonight."

What I saw through the window, sent a cold shiver down my spine. Jack must have seen the look of horror on my face because he jumped out of his chair and hurried over to join me.

"How is Florence floating in the air like that?" he said.

"She isn't *floating*."

"Yes, she is! I can see her. Look."

"It looks like she's floating, but technically speaking, she's using the 'levitation' spell."

"I didn't think she knew how to do that."

"She doesn't. She didn't. She—err—"

"Apparently, she does. What's going on, Jill?"

"I have no idea, but I'm going to find out." I hurried out into the garden. "Florence Maxwell!"

"Yes, Mummy?" she said, rather sheepishly.

"What are you doing up there?"

"Practising the left tator spell, Mummy."

"Get back down here immediately."

"Okay." Her bottom lip began to quiver, as she lowered herself gently back to the ground. "Are you mad at me, Mummy?"

"No, I'm not mad at you, but I need you to tell me how you learned to do that."

"But I promised I wouldn't say anything."

"When Mummy or Daddy ask you a question, you know that you have to give them an honest answer, don't you?"

"Yes, Mummy."

"Good. So, who was it who showed you how to do that?" As if I didn't already know.

"Great Grandma."

"And when did she show you?"

"Just now."

"Great Grandma was here in the garden?"

"Yes. I showed her how Buddy could fetch the ball, and then she said that she was going to show me a new spell."

"What did I tell you, Florence? I said you weren't allowed to learn any new spells until you were older."

"Great Grandma said it would be alright."

"You mustn't use the left tator—err—'levitation' spell again."

"But why, Mummy? It's fun. It's like flying."

"Do you see this high fence? There's a river over the other side which is very dangerous. If you were to levitate over the fence, you might fall in the river and drown."

"Great Grandma said I wouldn't be able to go as high as the fence."

"Never mind what Great Grandma said. You aren't to use that spell again. Understood?"

"Yes, Mummy. I'm sorry."

"It's alright, darling. Come here and have a hug." She threw herself into my arms and I could feel her sobbing. I felt terrible for having a go at her, but she'd scared me to death. Just wait until I got hold of Grandma—she and I were going to fall out big time.

Chapter 8

The next morning, I was still seething about what had happened the day before.

"I don't understand how your grandmother did it," Jack said. "I was in the kitchen all the time. I would have seen her."

"You know what Grandma is like. She can be very crafty. She knew precisely what she was doing."

"How many spells does Florence know now?"

"Until yesterday, she only knew three: 'Take it back', 'magnet' and 'hide'. I asked her if Great Grandma had shown her any other spells, and she said that she hadn't."

"Do you believe her?"

"Yes, Florence wouldn't lie to me."

"What's your plan regarding your grandmother?"

"I'm going over there this morning, to have it out with her. I'll tell her straight that if she tries it on again, I'll forbid her from seeing Florence."

Jack shushed me. "I think Florence is coming downstairs."

Moments later, she ran into the room. "Mummy, I have to take some ribbon to school."

"What's it for?"

"I don't know. Miss Soap said we had to take some."

"Miss *Soap*?"

"It's Miss *Hope*," Jack said.

"Florence, why didn't you tell Mummy this yesterday?"

"I'm sorry. I forgot because I was playing with Buddy. Can you get me some ribbon, Mummy?"

"There isn't any in the house."

"Miss will be mad if I don't take some."

"Okay. Have your breakfast with Daddy, and I'll try to sort something out." I turned to Jack, and mouthed, "Aunt Lucy."

Aunt Lucy was clearly surprised to see me.

"Morning, Jill. You're bright and early. Is everything okay?"

"No—err—yes, everyone's fine. Do you happen to have any ribbon in the house?"

"Lots of it. What colour would you like?"

"I'm not sure. Florence is supposed to take some into school this morning, but she didn't tell me until a few minutes ago."

"Why don't you take a length of each one? That should cover it."

"That would be great, thanks."

While Aunt Lucy was cutting the ribbon, I told her what Grandma had done. She was every bit as angry as I was.

"That woman gets worse. How dare she go behind your back and do something like that? You must be livid."

"I am. It's not just that she showed Florence a new spell after I'd specifically told her not to, but of all the spells she could have chosen, it had to be that one. What was she thinking? I dread to think what could have happened if Florence had got over the fence. It doesn't bear thinking about."

"What are you going to do?"

"I'm going to have a word with Grandma, a very strong word. In fact, as soon as I've taken this ribbon to Florence, I'll pop back and have it out with her. There's no time like the present."

"I'm afraid you're out of luck. I saw her leave the house

early this morning."

"Any idea where she was going?"

"No, sorry."

"Not to worry. I'll catch up with her later."

***

When I arrived at the office, Mrs V was humming to herself and beaming from ear to ear.

"Good morning, Mrs V. You're looking particularly happy this morning. Have you won the lottery or something?"

"No, dear. I really shouldn't smile. I'm being very unfair."

"What's happened?"

"You know how Armi laughed at me when I was hit on the head with the acorn? Well, last night, I was looking through the kitchen window when Armi took out the rubbish. He was just on his way back to the house when he was hit on the head by an acorn." She dissolved into laughter.

"Mrs V, that's not very nice."

"You're right, dear, but it did feel a little like Karma."

"Those squirrels of yours sound positively dangerous."

"They are."

"What are you going to do about them?"

"I'm not sure. Do you think I should shoot them?"

"You mustn't do that, or you'll land yourself in a whole heap of trouble."

"You're right. Armi and I had better put our thinking caps on to see what we can come up with."

"Will you be able to wear caps with your poorly

heads?" I laughed.

"Not funny, Jill."

"Sorry. In other news, I bumped into our new neighbour from down the corridor."

"Is it a hairdresser?"

"Actually, no. She's a dog groomer."

"How lovely. That'll mean we'll have lots of cute dogs coming in and out."

"It'll certainly be an improvement on the clowns. And, talking of dogs, we have one now."

"Since when?"

"A couple of days ago. Florence has a little Chihuahua called Buddy."

"How lovely for her. Are the two of them getting on alright?"

"Florence loves Buddy to pieces."

"And Buddy?"

"He puts up with her. I think that's the best we can hope for."

"You'll be able to take Buddy to Bubbles."

"That lazy dog doesn't go outside long enough to get dirty."

Winky was sitting on my desk, and he had a face like thunder. Thankfully, though, there was no sign of the freaky eye patch.

"Good morning, Winky."

"What's good about it?" he snapped.

"What's wrong with you? Did you get out of bed on the wrong side this morning?"

"I'll tell you what's wrong with me. I'm not happy about having a dog groomer down the corridor."

"Why not?"

He rolled his eye. "In case you hadn't noticed, cats and dogs are sworn enemies. Having that place down the corridor will make my life very difficult."

"I don't see why. Most of the time you come and go through the window. Anyway, I'm pleased to see you've got rid of that horrible eye patch."

"I haven't. It's in the wash. In fact, I'm going to buy another three."

"The same as that freaky one?"

"Yes, but in different colours."

"But they're horrible."

"Says you."

***

Rather than have me travel around the country to interview her relatives, Caroline had insisted they come to the manor house. The first of those interviews was with Caroline's brother, Ransom Tyler, who Mulgrave always referred to as Mr Ransom.

Mulgrave met me at the door and led the way across the large hallway.

"Lady Tweaking has designated the Marble Room for your interviews, madam. It's to the rear of the property."

He opened the door onto what was a small, rather bland room.

"I don't see any marble, Mulgrave."

"There isn't any, madam. When the children were young, they used to play marbles in this room, and the name stuck. Do take a seat. Mr Ransom should be with you shortly."

I had a choice between a worn-out sofa or a couple of worn-out armchairs, so I opted for the one closest to the window, which was the best of a bad bunch. The room was slightly warmer than the hallway, but nowhere near as warm as the dining room where I'd met with Caroline on my previous visit.

I'd only been waiting for a few minutes when in walked a tall man who looked about the same age as Caroline. He had a pale complexion, striking blue eyes, and more than his fair share of hair.

"I assume you're Mrs Maxwell."

"That's right. Call me Jill. And you must be Mr Ransom?"

"It's Ransom. Just Ransom. Only Mulgrave calls me *Mr Ransom*."

"Thank you for agreeing to speak to me today."

"I didn't have much choice in the matter. I honestly don't know why it was necessary for me to drive halfway across the country for this meeting. Surely you could have come to me?"

"I'd have been more than happy to, but your sister —"

"I might have known this was her idea. Typical of her. Alright, I suppose we'd better crack on with this. What is it you want, exactly?"

"I'm trying to establish what happened to the Tweaking Goblet."

"And I assume my sister thinks I stole it, does she?"

"She's made no such suggestion to me. I'll be speaking to everyone who was present on the day it went missing. The day of the birthday celebrations."

"*Celebrations*?" he scoffed. "It was a miserable affair. I've had more fun at a wake."

"I believe you spent some time in the games room, playing billiards?"

"I did. Anything to get away from that boring, awful gossip. Dominic and I played a couple of games. I won of course."

"Did you happen to notice if the goblet was in the room at the time?"

"Yes, it was."

"Are you sure about that?"

"Positive."

"Caroline said she didn't have any idea why someone would want to steal the goblet. She called it ugly and of little value. Can you think of any reason why someone should have taken it?"

"None at all. I don't often agree with my sister, but she's right about the goblet. It's a grotesque thing that can't be worth more than a couple of hundred pounds as scrap. Personally, I wouldn't give it house room. Whoever took it is welcome to it. I can't imagine why she's wasting good money, hiring you to try and find it. It's not as though she has money to spare. Just look at the state of this place. It's an absolute disgrace. My parents would turn in their grave if they could see what had happened to this magnificent building."

"I understand the family has had a few financial problems."

"That's the understatement of the decade, and it's all my sister's fault. If I'd inherited the estate, this would never have happened."

***

I'd no sooner left Tweaking Manor than I received a text from Aunt Lucy, which simply read, 'Grandma is home.'

Right! It was time for a showdown.

I magicked myself over to her house and knocked loudly on the door.

"What's all that noise about? I'm not deaf, you know!"

"I'd like a word with you."

"I'm rather busy at the moment."

"I don't care. This is important."

"Very well, then. I was just about to make myself a cup of tea. You can put the kettle on."

"I don't have time for a drink. We need to talk."

"This had better be good." She sighed. "What's so important that you're keeping me away from my cup of tea?"

"You came over to our house yesterday and showed Florence how to use the 'levitation' spell."

"What of it?"

"I thought we'd agreed you wouldn't show her any more spells. Don't you realise how dangerous it could have been if she'd levitated herself over the fence and fallen into the river?"

"Don't be ridiculous, Jill. I deliberately made sure that she wouldn't be able to get as high as the fence. I'm not stupid, you know."

"This simply isn't on, Grandma. If you can't respect my wishes, not to teach Florence any more spells, I will forbid you from seeing her."

"Forbid me!" she scoffed. "And how exactly would you do that?"

It was a good question; how would I stop her?

"I just don't understand why you insist on doing it, Grandma."

"Because, young lady, I think you're making a very serious mistake by restricting your daughter's access to magic."

"That's for Jack and me to decide, not you."

"What's that human got to do with it?"

"That human is my husband. And Florence's father."

Until Florence was born, the only person who'd known that Jack knew I was a sup was Daze. When my daughter came along, I bit the bullet and told my immediate 'sup' family: Grandma, Aunt Lucy and the twins. They were, of course, all sworn to secrecy.

"Have you forgotten how you felt when you discovered that you'd been a witch all your life but hadn't known?"

"That's different."

"How is it different?"

"Because I — err — because it just is."

"That's a very compelling argument. Can't you see you're doing exactly the same thing to Florence? She's going to grow up not understanding what it is to be a witch."

"She already knows she's part human, part witch."

"A witch who isn't allowed to learn magic isn't a witch."

"It's important for her to settle into the human world first. Then, when she's older —"

"That's nonsense," Grandma interrupted. "The girl must be allowed to be a witch right now. If you wait, it will be far more difficult for her to adapt. Just like it was for you. You don't even allow her to come to Candlefield."

"Yes, but—"

"But what? Why won't you let her visit the paranormal world? She's a sup, Jill. She should spend time in both worlds. You're not being fair to the child."

"I'm only trying to do what's best for her."

"I know you are, but you're failing her. Just think about it. If you continue on this road, what will happen when her invitation from CASS arrives on your doorstep?"

"I hadn't even thought about that."

"Well, you should. It's obvious that any daughter of yours is bound to be invited to attend CASS."

"I'm not even sure I'd want her to go there."

"Are you serious?" Grandma snapped. "Are you telling me that if Florence received an invitation from the most prestigious school in the paranormal world, you'd deny her that opportunity?"

"No—err—yes—err, I don't know. I haven't thought about it."

"It strikes me that you haven't thought about any of this. I suggest you go away and give it very careful consideration."

"Okay, I'll—err—I'll have another chat with Jack."

"That human should have no say in it."

"Jack is Florence's father. We'll decide together."

"Just make sure you come to the right decision. You don't want your daughter growing up to resent you, do you?"

Chapter 9

I left Grandma's house feeling dazed and confused. The encounter had not gone at all as I'd expected. I'd gone in there, all guns blazing, but by the time I left, I had to admit that some of the points she'd made were valid.

I was still standing outside her house, in something of a daze, when Aunt Lucy called to me, "Jill, are you okay?"

"I'm fine."

"Are you sure? You don't look it. Why don't you come inside, and I'll make you a cup of tea?"

"Okay, thanks."

While Aunt Lucy made the drinks, I told her everything that Grandma had said.

"You probably don't want to hear this, Jill, but I think your grandmother may have a point."

"So do I. That's the problem. I was convinced that we were doing the best thing for Florence. We just want to protect her."

"Of course you do. Everyone understands that, including your grandmother. None of this can be easy for you or Jack. The last thing I want to do is make this even more difficult for you, but I'd be less than honest if I didn't say that it would be lovely if Florence could visit us here in Candlefield."

"I know. I'd love to bring her over, but is it the right thing to do? The right thing for Florence, I mean?"

"Only you and Jack can make that decision."

"I'm going to talk it through with him tonight."

Aunt Lucy handed me the tea. "Why don't we go outside, and sit in the back garden? It's a lovely day. It might help to clear your head."

"Okay."

We took our drinks outside and sat on the bench.

"The garden is looking fabulous, Aunt Lucy."

"Thanks. It ought to be after all the time I spend in here these days."

Two years earlier, Aunt Lucy's neighbours, the Bees, had moved to a larger property, to accommodate their growing family. Not long afterwards, Charlie Roundtree, a wizard, had moved in next door. Retired and a widower, Charlie was a mad keen gardener, and it had been his influence that had re-sparked Aunt Lucy's interest in gardening.

I took a sip of tea. "Didn't you say you were going to enter a competition this year?"

"That's right: Candlefield in Bloom. The judging takes place at the end of next week, so I'm starting to get nervous."

"You must be in with a great chance. Those flower beds are absolutely stunning."

"I appreciate you saying that, but it's nowhere near as good as Charlie's." She gestured to the house next door. "Take a look."

I got up from the bench, walked over to the dividing wall, and looked at next door's garden.

"That's beautiful too. There's nothing to choose between them, in my opinion. It'll be difficult for the judges to pick a winner."

By the time I'd finished my tea, my head had cleared a little, and I felt ready to return to the office.

***

As I made my way up the stairs, I could hear voices coming from the outer office. Talking to Mrs V was Jules, who I hadn't seen for almost a year. She had a young baby in her arms.

"Jules, how lovely to see you."

"Hi, Jill. I hope you don't mind me calling in like this."

"Not at all. You're welcome to pop in anytime. And this little darling must be Harry. He's gorgeous."

And for once, I wasn't lying. Harry really was a handsome little boy.

"Gorgeous he may be." Jules managed a half-hearted laugh. "But he's a little monkey. He never sleeps. I can't remember the last time I slept for more than two hours at a stretch."

"I know what that feels like, but trust me, it will pass."

"I do hope so. I'm exhausted."

"Have you decided if you'll be returning to work, Jules?"

"Not straight away. Dexter and I talked about it and we decided to wait until Harry's at school. Talking of which, has Florence started school yet?"

"Yeah, she has."

"Is she enjoying it?"

"So far, yes. Fingers crossed that continues."

"What about Jack? Is he still working from home?"

"Yes, and that's made all the difference. He's able to take Florence to school and pick her up every day." My phone rang. "Speak of the devil, it's Jack. I'd better take this. It was lovely to see you again, Jules. And you, Harry."

I went through to my office. "Jack? Is Florence okay?"

"She's fine. I rang to tell you the boiler packed up a couple of hours ago."

"Great! What's wrong with it?"

"I don't know. I tried switching it off and on again, but that didn't work."

"My husband, the technical genius."

"I've got a guy coming over in about an hour. Is there any chance you could pick Florence up from school? I need to stay in for the boiler man."

"Sure, no problem. I'll call it a day now and go straight over there."

***

Florence's school, Tweaking Juniors, was located at the opposite end of the village to the old watermill. A small school, with less than a hundred pupils, it served Middle Tweaking, Lower Tweaking and Higher Tweaking. Jack and I had both been very impressed when we'd looked around prior to Florence starting there.

Understandably, the school authorities did their best to dissuade parents from parking their cars near to the school, so I left mine outside our house, and made my way across the village on foot. When I arrived at the school, there were already several other parents waiting by the gates. By far the majority of them were mums, but there were a couple of dads there too. I'd only been standing there for a few minutes when a woman, about my age, came over and introduced herself.

"Hi, I'm Julie. I've not seen you here before."

"I'm Jill. I'm here to pick up my daughter, Florence Maxwell."

"Oh? Jack isn't poorly, is he?"

"Err, no, he's fine. He had to stay home because our boiler broke down this morning. He's waiting for the repairman."

"Boilers can be such a nuisance, can't they? We had to replace ours a few months ago. It cost an arm and a leg."

"Hopefully, it won't come to that."

"Your husband is such a lovely man. He's always making us laugh. My little boy, Gary, is in the same class as Florence. They're really good friends. She's probably mentioned him to you."

"Err, yeah, Gary. Of course." Had Florence mentioned his name? I couldn't be sure.

Another woman came to join us.

"Are you Jill Maxwell?"

"That's me."

"Jack is always talking about you. I'm Carol by the way. Kylie's my little girl. Florence must have mentioned her to you. The two of them are as thick as thieves."

"Kylie? Err, yes, of course. Nice to meet you."

"Jack's not ill, is he?"

"No, he's had to stay in for the boiler repairman."

"Jack is such a lovely man. You're so very lucky."

"I am."

A bell rang inside the building and a few moments later, there was a clicking sound as the iron gates opened. We all made our way along the path to the reception building where the kids were waiting with their teachers. As each child spotted their mum or dad, they rushed across the room to join them. I couldn't see Florence at first, but then she appeared, carrying something weird looking.

"Mummy, look what I've made."

"That's lovely, darling. It's a fantastic — err — spider?"

"It's not a spider, Mummy. It's an octopus."

"Oh yes, of course it is."

The legs of the spider/octopus had clearly been made from the ribbons that Aunt Lucy had given me that morning.

"Do you really like it, Mummy?"

"I do. It's amazing."

"Where's Daddy? Why didn't he come to get me?"

"He had to stay at home because the heating has broken."

"Is it cold in the house?"

"I haven't actually been home yet, but I wouldn't think so. Anyway, the repairman will be coming soon."

I was so busy chatting to Florence that I didn't notice the approach of a young woman until she was standing beside us.

"Hi, I'm Florence's teacher." She was wearing a sensible cardigan and skirt, and very sensible shoes. Even her hair, which was taken up into a bun, was sensible.

"Miss Soap?"

"It's Miss Hope, actually."

"Sorry, that's what I meant. Florence was just showing me her spider — err — octopus."

"All of the children have made different animals using ribbon. Florence's octopus is very good, isn't it?"

"It's fabulous. She's very clever."

"Is Jack poorly?"

"No, he's fine. He had to stay in because the boiler is on the blink."

"Right, I'd better get going. It was nice to meet you."

On the walk back through the village, Florence talked nonstop, telling me about the different animals that everyone else in her class had made.

"No one had as many different colours of ribbon as I had, Mummy."

"Your octopus is brilliant. Just wait until Daddy sees it."

When we arrived at the house, the boiler repairman's van was parked behind my car. As soon as we were inside, Florence went running over to Jack.

"Look what I've made, Daddy."

"That's a lovely octopus, darling." He gave her a hug.

How on Earth had he known it was an octopus? It definitely looked more like a spider.

"Good news, Jill. The man says it won't be a big job to mend the boiler."

"Thank goodness."

"Where's Buddy, Daddy?" Florence pulled on Jack's trouser leg.

"He's out in the garden."

"I'm going to play ball with him." She ran outside.

"Did everything go alright at the school, Jill?" Jack said.

"Fine. I've just spent the last ten minutes talking to your fan club."

"What do you mean?" He laughed.

"I was only standing outside the school gates for a few minutes, and two mums came over to ask where you were, and if you were okay. Then, when I got inside the school, Miss Soap, Hope, or whatever her name is, also seemed very concerned about you."

"What can I tell you?" He grinned. "I'm a popular guy."

"Apparently. Did the man say how much the repair

would be?"

"He reckons it shouldn't cost much more than fifty quid."

"That's good."

"Mummy!" Florence came running back into the house, clearly upset about something.

"What's the matter, darling?"

"Buddy won't fetch the ball."

"Are you sure? Have you thrown it for him a few times?"

"Yes, but he just stands there. I think he forgot how to do it."

"Okay. You stay here with Daddy, and I'll go and have a word with Buddy."

The Chihuahua was sitting on the path, giving me the evil eye.

"Hey, Buddy, I thought we'd agreed that you were going to play ball with Florence."

"Yes, but if you remember, part of that agreement was that you were going to provide me with the food I'd requested. And yet, today, all I've had to eat is that same old slop."

"We've not had a chance to go to the supermarket yet."

"And that's my problem, why?"

"Come on. If you play with her today, we'll make sure you get the new food tomorrow."

"No way. I played with her yesterday as a gesture of goodwill, but if you want me to do it again today, you'll have to come up with the goods."

It was clear there would be no persuading him, so I went back into the house.

"Where's Florence gone?" I said.

"She's just nipped upstairs to the loo."

"Buddy is refusing to play with her until he gets the new dog food. Why don't you pop to the supermarket to get it? I'll stay here with Florence, and I'll see to the boiler man."

"Okay." He grabbed his car keys. "I'll be as quick as I can."

A few minutes later, Florence came running down the stairs. "Mummy, Auntie Kathy is here with Lizzie."

"Are you sure?"

"I saw them through the window."

Sure enough, moments later, there was a knock at the front door.

"I hope you don't mind us calling around unannounced like this?" Kathy was standing there with Lizzie by her side. "I had to pick this one up from her friend's house. She lives not far from here, so I thought we'd pop in for a cup of tea if there's one on offer."

"Sure. Come on in. You've just missed Jack. He's gone to buy dog food."

"Since when did you have a dog?"

"Since a couple of days ago. It was Jack's bright idea. By the time I found out about it, it was a fait accompli."

"Lizzie, come and see Buddy." Florence took Lizzie by the hand. "He's in the garden."

The kids disappeared out of the house, and Kathy walked over to the window. "A Chihuahua. How sweet."

"There's nothing sweet about that dog."

"What do you mean?"

"I'm only kidding." Not!

The two girls didn't stay outside for very long because Buddy was still on strike.

"Come and see my bedroom, Lizzie," Florence said. "I want to show you the octopus I made at school."

"Okay, but let me show Auntie Jill my charm bracelet first." She held out her hand.

"That's — err — lovely."

"Mum bought it for me last weekend, didn't you, Mum?"

"Yes, under protest." Kathy rolled her eyes.

Florence grabbed Lizzie's hand, and the two of them disappeared upstairs.

"I'm surprised you bought her a bracelet. I didn't think you approved of her having jewellery."

"I resisted for as long as I could, but all the girls in her class have got them. Lizzie has been pestering me for ages to buy her one, so I said she could have it as a reward for being made captain of the netball team. They're a right scam. The bracelets are cheap enough, but the charms are really expensive. I've told Lizzie that if she wants any more charms, she'll have to save her pocket money, or have them for her birthday or Christmas."

Just then, I heard the front door open.

"You'll never believe it, Jill," Jack shouted. "I didn't need to go all the way to the supermarket. Incredibly, they had Buddy's food at Tweaking Stores. Now that's sorted, I suppose we'd better discuss whether or not we should let our little witch learn any more spells."

He walked into the room, saw Kathy, and his face fell.

"*Little witch?*" Kathy looked puzzled.

Fast on his feet as always, Jack stood there with his mouth wide open.

"It's something Florence is doing at school." I jumped in. "They have to dress up as mythical creatures, and I suggested she could be a witch."

"Why would she want to be a witch?" Kathy said. "They're ugly. Florence would make a much better fairy."

"You're probably right. Nothing's been decided yet, has it, Jack?"

"Err, no. I'll go and feed the dog, shall I?"

"Good idea."

Chapter 10

The next morning, on my drive to work, I reflected on the discussion that Jack and I had had the previous night. After Florence had gone to bed, I'd told him that Grandma had said we were being unfair by not allowing her to practise magic. I also revealed my own concerns that our decision might have an adverse effect on her later in life. It was only when I'd mentioned the possibility that Florence might be invited to attend CASS that Jack had become really animated. He'd been horrified at the idea, and his initial reaction had been that no daughter of his would ever go to a boarding school. Eventually, he'd calmed down and we'd managed to discuss the subject rationally. I told him that, although I couldn't bear the idea of Florence going to boarding school either, it was probably something that she should be allowed to decide for herself when the time came.

We agreed to put the subject of CASS on hold for the time being. Far more pressing was the question of if we should allow Florence to learn more magic now or stick to our original plan and wait until she was older. We also discussed the possibility of Florence going to Candlefield with me occasionally. Jack didn't have any objections to that, but I could tell he was saddened by the realisation that this was a part of her life he would never be able to share.

It was after midnight when we'd eventually decided to call it a day. We still hadn't made any concrete decisions, but I'd suggested it might be helpful if I could speak to someone who had been in the same position, to see what decisions they'd made, and how it had worked out for them. I'd come up with the idea of contacting the headmistress at CASS. I was sure there must be pupils at the school who came from a similar background.

Before I got out of the car in Washbridge, I made a call to CASS. I hadn't yet met the current headmistress, Hildegard Bogart, and I expected to have to leave a message, asking if she would call me back. As it turned out, as soon as I told the receptionist my name, I was put straight through.

"Jill Maxwell? This is Hildegard Bogart speaking. I have a note in my diary to give you a call soon, but you've saved me the trouble."

"Thank you for speaking to me, Headmistress. I was hoping to make an appointment to come over and talk to you sometime?"

"You can pop over now if you like."

"Are you sure that's convenient?"

"Absolutely."

"Great. I'll be with you in a few minutes."

I magicked myself straight over there.

"That was jolly quick, Jill." Ms Bogart cut a commanding figure. Tall and solid, she was much younger than Desdemona Nightowl. "Come in. Come in. I do hope you'll let me in on your secret spell."

"Sorry?"

"The one that allows you to magic yourself between Candlefield and CASS. I hate those dreadful airships."

"I'd be more than happy to show you, Headmistress, but I'm afraid the spell only seems to work for me."

"How very disappointing. Do have a seat. Can I get you a drink?"

"No, thanks. I'm afraid I can't stay long."

"I do hope you've come to tell me that you'd like to resume your teaching duties."

"I'm afraid not. At least not at the moment. My daughter, Florence, has only just started school. Maybe when she's a little older."

"How old is she? Five?"

"That's right."

"Such a lovely age."

"I want to make sure she's settled before I take on any more commitments. I hope you understand?"

"Of course, but please bear us in mind when circumstances allow, won't you?"

"Definitely. I really enjoyed my time here with the kids."

"It won't be too long until your daughter joins us here at CASS. It's surprising how fast the years fly by."

"Surely that will depend on whether or not she receives an invitation."

"I shouldn't really say this, but I think that's pretty much a formality. Anyway, what can I do for you today?"

"I'm here concerning Florence. You may not be aware, but my husband Jack is a human."

"I had no idea. That must make life very difficult. Does Florence know she's a witch?"

"Of course. I've never tried to hide that from her."

"Aren't you worried she might say something to your husband?"

"No. She knows it's our little secret. My problem is that I'm unsure how much magic I should teach her at this age. I had planned to keep it to a minimum until she was older, but my grandmother, Mirabel Millbright —"

"Mirabel? She's your grandmother?"

"That's right."

"I should have realised. Sorry to interrupt. You were saying?"

"I'd intended to wait until Florence was older before teaching her any more spells, but my grandmother is firmly of the opinion that I should be doing it now. That's why I'm here today. I'm hoping that I might be able to speak to pupils who are in a similar position—who have one parent who is a human and one who is a sup."

"That could be difficult."

"Oh? I assumed you'd have a few pupils who fell into that category."

"We don't, and there's a very good reason for that. The human parent would naturally expect to be able to look around the boarding school that their child is about to attend, but that's impossible."

"What a mess."

"As it happens, we do have one child from the human world with us at the moment. Maxine Pearldiver's mother is a witch and her father is a human."

"How did they manage to get around the issue you've just highlighted?"

"Her parents split up shortly after Maxine was born, leaving her mother to raise her alone. Her father simply disappeared and has played no part in her upbringing, so the decision to send Maxine to CASS was her mother's alone."

"I see. Would it be possible for me to speak to Maxine?"

"I'm sorry, Jill, but I can't allow you to do that without first getting permission from her mother. I'm sure you understand."

"Of course. In that case, would you be able to let me have her mother's contact details?"

"Unfortunately, I can't do that either—data protection and all that stuff. What I can do, though, is contact Maxine's mother on your behalf. I'll explain the situation and see if she's willing to talk to you. If she is, I'll ask her to get in touch with you directly. Is that okay?"

"That would be great. I hope she agrees but I'll understand if she'd rather not. I really do appreciate your time and help, Headmistress."

"My pleasure. And I hope to see you teaching here again soon."

***

I magicked myself back to the office.

"Good morning, Mrs V, how are you?"

"Fine, thanks." She sighed.

"Are you sure? You don't sound it."

"It's just those pesky squirrels."

"Are they still causing you problems?"

"It's getting worse. It's got to the point where Armi and I daren't go into the back garden because every time we do, we get pelted with acorns."

"Oh dear." Somehow, I managed not to laugh. "What are you going to do about it?"

"I've no idea. I called the pest control people, but they said that squirrels aren't considered to be pests. Those in my back garden certainly are."

There was something about this situation that just didn't ring true. Squirrels were normally such harmless, timid creatures. Could they really be behind the acorn attacks? Or was something more sinister afoot? Was it possible that the wood nymphs had returned?

In my office, Winky was talking to two cats who were seated on the sofa.

"Ah, she's here now. Jill, could you let us have some salmon, please. Red, obviously."

The cheek of that cat. He thought he could invite whoever he wanted, whenever he wanted, and that I'd just feed them. Well, enough was enough.

"Could I have a word, Winky?" I beckoned him over to the opposite side of the room, and then said in a whisper, "You can't just invite your friends in here and expect me to feed them. It's not on. Tell them they have to leave."

"They aren't my friends."

"That makes it even worse. You can't invite strangers in for a free meal."

"They're cops. They're working undercover."

"Pull the other one. I'm not stupid."

He turned to the two cats. "Would you mind introducing yourselves to Jill?"

"We really shouldn't," the male cat said. "This is an undercover operation as we explained to you."

"This is Jill's office. She won't say anything, will you?"

"I — err — . No, of course not."

"Okay." The cat flipped open a wallet and flashed a badge at me. "Agent Ricardo, CI5."

"CI5?"

"Officer Lulu." The female cat showed me an identical badge.

"What's this all about?"

"We're running surveillance on the building opposite."

She gestured to the window. "This room gives us the optimum vantage point."

"What's going on over there?"

"We're not at liberty to divulge that information, but suffice to say, it involves organised crime."

"I see. How long will you need to be here?"

"Hard to say. We hope to be out by the end of next week."

"End of next week?"

"Hopefully. Is that okay?"

"I — err — guess so."

"Now, about that salmon," Winky said.

"Err, sure. Coming right up."

***

I was paying another visit to Tweaking Manor, this time to speak to Caroline's sister, Elizabeth Judge. Mulgrave met me at the door and led the way to the Marble Room where Elizabeth Judge was already waiting. If I hadn't known the two women were sisters, I never would have guessed. The contrast between them was remarkable: Caroline seemed to care very little about her appearance. Her sister, on the other hand, looked as though she was ready to pose for a fashion shoot. Her clothes were well tailored and clearly extremely expensive, and she was dripping in jewellery. Her makeup and hair were both immaculate.

"Thank you for seeing me, Mrs Judge," I said.

"Call me Elizabeth, please, and it's my pleasure. I'm happy to do whatever I can to help my sister." She turned to the butler. "Mulgrave, would you be kind enough to make us a drink? Is tea alright for you, Jill?"

"Tea's fine, thanks."

"Very well, madam," Mulgrave said, and then he left the room.

"I do apologise that we had to meet in this dreadful room, Jill. It's so cold in here. I had hoped we might be able to use the dining room, which is much warmer, but it seems that my sister has a meeting in there with her lawyer."

"That's okay. I'm perfectly fine in here." As long as I kept brushing the icicles off my nose.

"I assume you want to discuss the missing goblet."

"That's right. I've already spoken to your brother about it."

"Between you and me, you need look no further than Ransom to solve this particular mystery."

"I'm not sure I understand. Are you suggesting that it was your brother who stole the goblet?"

"I'm not *suggesting* it. I'm saying it loud and clear."

"What reason could he have for doing that? As I understand it, the goblet has no real value."

"It doesn't, but this is just the sort of thing he would do. He's an idiot. He's always been an idiot. If you've spoken to him, you must surely have reached the same conclusion. I'm ashamed to call him my brother. He and Dominic were playing billiards in the games room that night. He probably waited until Dominic had left the room and then grabbed the goblet."

"I knew Ransom had been playing billiards, but according to your sister, she checked the games room just before she turned in for the night, and she's adamant the goblet was still in there."

"That's as maybe, but I still think Ransom's behind this. He has a massive chip on his shoulder."

"About what?"

"He believes that he should be lord of the manor, but as Caroline has no doubt told you, the title doesn't actually exist. Our father left the house and grounds to Caroline, and that's what really riles Ransom. Father knew what Ransom was like and that he'd probably sell off the house to fund the lifestyle he aspires to."

"I see. When I spoke to him, he was clearly unhappy at the current state of Tweaking Manor."

"That's understandable. We all are. None of us enjoys seeing the house in this state of disrepair, but I honestly don't know what he expects my sister to do about it. She can't magic money out of thin air." Elizabeth managed a weak smile. "What we really need is for the Tweaking legend to prove to be true."

"What legend is that?"

"Has no one told you about the parchment?"

"No."

"In that case, you'd better come with me, and I'll show you."

We bumped into Mulgrave on our way out of the door.

"Mulgrave, would you be a dear and pour out the tea?" Elizabeth said. "I'm just taking Jill to see the parchment."

"Very well, madam."

Elizabeth led the way back to the hallway, and then down yet another corridor.

"This is the Cedar Room." She opened the door onto an empty room. "As you can see, it's no longer in use. The parchment is over there on the wall."

I walked over to get a closer look. The parchment had

been mounted behind glass in a wooden frame. The writing was faded, but I could just about make out the words, which I read out loud, "The first one to unlock the vault. And find riches beyond your wildest dreams." I turned to Elizabeth. "Is it okay if I take a photo of this?"

"Of course."

I snapped a photo with my phone. "Is there a vault in this house?"

"Not that anyone is aware of. If you ask me, the parchment is no more than a practical joke, played on us by one of our ancestors. It's a shame because, goodness knows, the family could do with the treasure. Between you and me, if my sister doesn't come up with the money to pay the tax bill soon, she'll lose the house, and that would be a tragedy."

Chapter 11

I was beginning to flag, so I magicked myself over to Cuppy C for a coffee and a blueberry muffin. As I approached the counter, I spotted Daze and Blaze seated by the window. They were deep in conversation and hadn't even noticed me come into the shop.

"Hi, Jill." Pearl was by herself behind the counter.

"Hi. Can I get a caramel latte and a blueberry muffin, please?"

"Coming up."

"Those two look busy."

"They've been like that for the last half hour. I don't think either of them is in a particularly good mood."

I had my drink and muffin, and I was just about to take a seat at another table when Daze spotted me. "Jill, come and join us."

"Are you sure? You look busy."

"We're busy alright." She sighed. "But never too busy to talk to you. Come and sit down."

"Okay, thanks. You both look stressed out. What's going on?"

"You might well ask," Blaze said. "Things have gone from crazy to ridiculous."

"We're working on the Romeo case," Daze said.

"*Romeo*? Who's that?"

"I'm surprised you haven't heard of him. He's a wizard, and a thoroughly nasty piece of work. They call him Romeo because he's a bit of a ladies' man, or at least he thinks he is." She took a photo out of her pocket and passed it to me.

"Romeo? Seriously? He's no oil painting, is he? Why are

you after him?"

"He's been in and out of prison in Candlefield for as long as I can remember. He's supposed to be out on licence at the moment, but he's gone missing."

"What was he in prison for?"

"Bank robberies. Dozens of them. He has the unusual distinction of being loathed equally by the authorities and his fellow criminals."

"Why would his fellow criminals loathe him?"

"He works with a different accomplice every time, and he thinks nothing of doing the dirty on his partner-in-crime."

"How do you mean?"

"They commit the crime together, and then he disappears with the money, leaving his unwitting accomplice to carry the can."

"Are you saying he plans for that to happen?"

"Definitely. It's happened too often for it to be a coincidence. There's no sign of him in Candlefield, and my bosses believe he may have moved his operation to the human world."

"Is that likely?"

"It's possible. He probably can't find anyone who'll work with him here because of his reputation."

"Which of course no one would be aware of in the human world?"

"Correct."

I held out the photograph.

"Hang onto it, just in case. I've got plenty more."

"That's not the only case we're working on," Blaze blurted out. "The black market for A-Juice has gone crazy as well."

"A-Juice?"

Before either of them could elaborate, Daze's phone rang. "You've got to be kidding me." She spat the words into the phone. "Why does that involve us? Okay. Okay. Yes, yes, we'll come in now."

"What was all that about?" Blaze said when she'd finished on the call.

"We've got to go to HQ straight away."

"Why? What's happened now?"

"Apparently, there have been numerous missing person reports."

"What do they expect us to do? We're busy enough already."

"Don't you think I know that?" Daze stood up, her face red with rage. "But you know what they say. If you want something doing, ask a busy woman. Sorry, Jill, we have to go."

"Good luck with everything."

***

I'd no sooner magicked myself back to Washbridge, than my phone rang. I didn't recognise the caller ID; that usually meant it was either a personal injury lawyer touting for business, or someone peddling an unmissable investment opportunity. I was all set to tell them where to shove it when the female caller said, "Jill Maxwell? This is Freda Pearldiver."

Although Freda's situation wasn't exactly the same as mine, I still believed her experience might inform my decisions regarding Florence. And, hopefully, she would give me permission to speak to her daughter, Maxine.

"Freda? Thanks for calling. I didn't expect to hear from you so soon."

"The headmistress at CASS told me that you'd spoken to her. She said you thought it would help to talk to me."

"That's right. I'd like to come and see you if you can spare me the time."

"I'd be more than happy to talk to you, Jill, but I have plans for the rest of the day. How about tomorrow afternoon? Does that work for you?"

"That would be great."

"Okay. I'll text you my address now. Shall we say one o'clock?"

"Yeah. I'll see you then."

It was clear that the police had dismissed Rusty's report of a shooting as no more than the fanciful imagination of someone they considered to be a time-wasting nuisance.

I wanted to take a look at the properties on the other side of the park, where the alleged shooting had taken place. As it was such a lovely day, I left my car on the street where Rusty lived and took a walk through the park. It was very quiet in there. In fact, I only encountered two people: The first, a middle-aged jogger who was running so slowly that I overtook him, even though I was only walking. The second, a woman in her mid-fifties, was walking five poodles. Surely five poodles were too many poodles for anyone.

Even from the rear of the properties, I could tell that the houses were very similar to the one in which Rusty lived. The tall fence and streetlights that bordered the park would have made it very difficult for anyone to gain access to those houses without being noticed. I followed the fence until I came to another gate.

I didn't plan on calling at the house where the alleged shooting had taken place because by all accounts, the occupants had been rather upset when the police had called on them to discuss the so-called incident. I figured if I turned up on their doorstep, that would only stir up even more ill feeling towards Rusty. Instead, I intended to focus on the properties on either side.

I started with the house to the left. I'd no sooner pressed the bell, than the door flew open. A young boy, no more than eight years old, was standing there. He had chocolate all around his mouth and even on his nose.

"Hello?" he said. "I'm Roger."

"I'm very pleased to meet you, Roger. Is your mummy or daddy in?"

"Daddy's at work. He's a solicitor."

"Is your mummy in?"

"She's in the kitchen, making buns. She let me eat some chocolate cream out of the bowl."

"Do you think I could have a word with her, Roger?"

"Who is it?" The female voice came from the back of the house.

"It's a lady, Mummy."

"What does she want?"

"What do you want?" Roger asked me.

"I'd like to talk to your mummy for a few minutes."

"She says she wants to talk to you for a few minutes."

His mother was wearing an apron covered in flour and chocolate cream.

"If you're selling anything, I'm afraid we don't buy at the door." Was her opening gambit.

"I'm not selling anything."

"Roger, go and wash your face. You've got chocolate all over it." She ushered him away. "If you aren't selling anything, what do you want?"

"My name is Jill Maxwell. I'm a private investigator."

"Was it my husband you wanted to see? He's at work at the moment."

"No, I'm sure you'll be able to answer my questions."

"About what?"

"I'm investigating an alleged shooting that happened last week."

"A *shooting*?" She looked shocked. "Around here?"

"There was a report of a shooting in the house next door."

"Now I come to think of it, I did see a police car out front a few days ago. I just assumed there'd been another burglary. We've had a few around here recently. Was someone shot?"

"The police don't seem to think so. In fact, when they spoke to your neighbours, they were told that no such shooting had taken place."

"In that case, why are you here?"

"I'm working for the gentleman who witnessed the incident."

"Who's that?"

"I'm not at liberty to disclose his name, but he lives in one of the houses on the opposite side of the park."

"And he reckons he saw a shooting from that distance away?"

"That's right. I take it you didn't hear anything unusual?"

"No, and if there had been a gunshot, we would definitely have heard it because these walls are awfully thin. The only thing we hear from next door is their incessant arguing."

"Do they argue a lot?"

"All the time."

"Can you tell me anything else about your neighbours?"

"Not really. They moved in about three years ago. Since then, I've probably spoken to them no more than half a dozen times, and then only to say hello. They aren't particularly sociable and to be honest, neither are we. In fact, everyone around here tends to keep themselves to themselves. Look, I really do have to get back to my baking."

"Of course. Thank you very much for your time."

So far, it wasn't looking good for Rusty, but I wasn't one to give up easily, so I moved to the house next door but one. This time, when I rang the doorbell, a window on the first floor opened, and an elderly man stuck his head out.

"Are you the blind woman?"

That struck me as a curious question. "Err, no."

"Are you sure? The man in the shop said the woman would be here to measure for the blinds about thirty minutes ago. Stay there. I'm coming down."

I heard footsteps on the stairs and then the door opened. "Are you sure you're not the blind woman?"

"Positive."

"Have you seen her?"

"No, sorry."

"Whatever happened to punctuality? That's what I'd like to know." He tapped his watch. "Thirty minutes I've been waiting for her. It really isn't good enough. If you aren't here to measure for the blinds, why are you here?"

"My name's Jill Maxwell. I'm a private investigator."

"*Private investigator?*" He looked me up and down. "Are you sure?"

"I'm positive."

"Well, I never. I didn't realise that women could do that kind of thing."

"You'd be surprised what women can do."

"What is it you're investigating, young lady?"

"There's been a report of a shooting in the house next door."

"Good gracious? Are you sure?"

"Apparently, it was witnessed by someone who lives in one of the properties at the other side of the park."

"How on Earth did they see it from over there? I can barely make out those houses from here."

"Can I take it that you didn't hear anything unusual from next door?"

"No, just the usual arguments. Those two are always going at it. It never stops. I wouldn't be surprised if one of them did shoot the other one. To be honest, it would be a blessing. How am I supposed to watch my cricket with all that racket going on?"

"Do you know your neighbours well?"

"I do not, and what's more, I have absolutely no desire to. I like to keep myself to myself."

"Can I ask, do you live here alone?"

"Yes. My wife, Jennifer, died fifteen years ago. Very inconsiderate of her if you ask me. I have to make my own meals now. It's such a nuisance. And this house doesn't keep itself tidy, you know. I don't suppose you're looking for a housekeeper's job, are you?"

"Me? No, sorry."

"Housekeepers are so difficult to come by, and even when you manage to get one, they only need the slightest excuse to leave. The last one complained because I left my dirty underwear on the bathroom floor."

Gross! "Right, okay, well thank you very much for your time."

"No problem, and if you happen to see the blind woman on your travels, would you tell her to get a move on?"

"Sure."

"If you change your mind about the housekeeper's job, come back and see me. The job's yours for the asking."

As I made my way back across the park, I was trying to figure out what to do about Rusty. If I told him that I was coming around to the police's view that he'd imagined the whole thing, he would be devastated. In the end, I decided not to tell him anything just yet. Not until I was one-hundred percent sure that he was mistaken.

I was halfway across the park when something hit me on top of the head.

"Ouch." I glanced down and saw the offending object: An acorn. Above me, perched on a branch was a squirrel; he was grinning. "Hey you!" I shouted. "What do you think you're doing? That hurt."

"It serves you right." He sneered.

"What do you mean, it serves me right? What did I ever do to you?"

"This is my territory. Go and find your own acorns."

"I wasn't looking for acorns. I was just walking through

the park, minding my own business when you threw one at me."

"That's what they all say. If you come around here again, you'll get more of that."

What a horrible creature. I was sorely tempted to do something unspeakable to him, but I turned the other cheek and carried on through the park. Maybe Mrs V wasn't as crazy as I'd thought she was. When she'd told me that she and Armi had come under attack from squirrels in their back garden, I'd thought she was nuts. Maybe, she'd been right all along. If so, why had the squirrel population suddenly turned to violence?

Chapter 12

It was Saturday morning, and Jack and I were in the kitchen, eating breakfast. Florence had already finished hers and was in the back garden, playing with Buddy.

When I'd finished eating, I took the bowl over to the sink, and glanced out of the window. "I'll need to have serious words with that dog."

"Why?" Jack looked up from his newspaper. "Is he refusing to play ball again?"

"He is fetching it, but instead of running after it like a normal dog, he just saunters up and down the garden at a snail's pace."

"Take a look at this, Jill." Jack pointed to the headlines on the front page of The Bugle, which he now had delivered every morning (for reasons that were beyond my comprehension). "There's been another bank robbery."

"Where?"

"In West Chipping. The MO sounds identical to the one in Washbridge. There were two robbers inside the bank, but only one of them was caught. The other one disappeared with all the money."

"And let me guess, there's no trace of him on CCTV?"

"That's right."

"I didn't mention this before because I wasn't sure if it was relevant, but I was talking to Daze and Blaze yesterday. They're up to their necks in cases at the moment, and one of them is a fugitive—a wizard who goes by the nickname of Romeo. He's been responsible for dozens of bank robberies in Candlefield."

"And you think he might have had something to do

with the recent ones?"

"Possibly. Apparently, he's earned himself a bad reputation amongst the criminal fraternity in the paranormal world."

"How come?"

"He has a habit of skipping the crime scene with all the money, leaving his partner to carry the can. Daze thinks it may have got to the point where no one in the paranormal world is willing to work with him."

"And she thinks he may have moved over here?"

"Yeah, and I'm going to try and help her to find him."

"How?"

"I have my methods."

***

When Florence was four years old, she decided she wanted to go to dance class. I'd tried my best to persuade her that she'd enjoy kickboxing, judo or karate much more, but she (and Jack) were having none of it. Several of her friends from nursery went to dance class, and she wanted to do the same. So, every Saturday morning, Jack or I (sometimes both of us) took her to the dance class, which was held in the village hall. This was the same building that for a short time had been home to the Middle Tweaking Theatre Company.

Although I like nothing better than to see Florence enjoying herself, there can't be many things that are more boring than watching a load of five-year-olds 'dancing' around a village hall. Particularly when that village hall is always cold.

"I really think she's starting to get the hang of it." Jack

pointed to Florence who was wearing a cute little tutu.

"She's doing great. Who's the big girl over there?"

All of the other girls and boys were about the same height as Florence, except this one girl who was at least two or three inches taller than the others. She was a werewolf which caught me by surprise because I hadn't encountered any other sups in Middle Tweaking.

"I don't know. I've not seen her here before. She must be new." Jack glanced around at the other parents. "There's a couple over there that I don't recognise. Maybe she's their daughter."

I followed his gaze, and sure enough the proud parents were both werewolves.

Florence cried out. I looked around, to see her lying on the floor, and was just about to run over to her, when she jumped up and said, "I'm alright, Mummy."

I turned to Jack. "What happened?"

"The big girl knocked her over. It was clearly an accident. She didn't mean to do it."

Ten minutes later, the young werewolf girl bumped into Florence again. This time, though, Florence managed to stay on her feet, and seemed totally unconcerned.

I was livid. I was sure the big girl had done it deliberately, and I wasn't going to stand for it.

"No, Jill!" Jack grabbed my arm.

"What?"

"You have that look on your face."

"I don't know what you're talking about."

"You can't use magic."

"I wasn't going to hurt her. I was just going to —"

"No! Do you hear me?"

"Okay." That husband of mine could be such a killjoy

sometimes.

***

When dance class had finally ended, the three of us made our way back home through the village.

"Are you sure you're okay, Florence?" I said. "That big girl didn't hurt you, did she?"

"No, Mummy. Wendy's my new friend. She said that one day I can go to her house to play with her dollies and her rat."

"She has a rat?"

"Yes, his name is Ratty. Can I have a milkshake please, Mummy?"

"We don't have any in the house."

"They sell them in there." She pointed to Tweaking Tea Rooms. "My friend, Jackie, says the milkshakes in there are the best in the world. Can we, please?"

I turned to Jack. "Have you been in there before?"

"No, but I don't see why we shouldn't treat ourselves. Are you okay for time?"

"Yeah. I don't have to be at Freda Pearldiver's until one o'clock."

"Come on, then." He took Florence's hand. "Let's go and get you that milkshake."

The small tea room was all brass kettles, lace curtains and doilies. We'd no sooner stepped through the door than a young woman, wearing a black dress and white apron, came scurrying over to us.

"Good morning. Welcome to Tweaking Tea Rooms. Would you like a window table? They're very popular, but we do have one free at the moment."

I glanced around at the empty shop.

"Yes, please, that would be great," Jack said.

We'd just sat down and hadn't even had a chance to pick up the menus before the waitress pounced. "What can I get for you?"

"Could you give us a minute while we decide?" I said.

"Err, yes, of course." She glanced nervously over her shoulder at a woman, seated on a stool in front of the counter. She had grey hair with purple highlights and looked quite ferocious.

I had assumed the waitress would come back once we'd had chance to decide what we wanted, but instead she continued to hover close by.

"Are you ready to order yet?"

I was just about to tell her to back off when Florence piped up, "I'd like a strawberry milkshake, please."

"Do you have those?" Jack asked.

"Yes, we do lots of different flavours of milkshake." The waitress glanced again over her shoulder.

She was beginning to freak me out, so I asked, "Is everything okay?"

After another quick glance over her shoulder, she leaned forward and whispered, "That's Miss Drinkwater, the boss, she gets annoyed if we don't take the orders quickly. I'm really sorry."

"It's okay. It's not your fault. I'll just have a cup of tea, please."

"Tea for me, too," Jack said.

"Would you like anything to eat?" the waitress asked.

"Can I have a bun, please, Mummy." Florence gave me that cute little smile of hers. The one I could never say no to.

"What kind of cakes do you have?" I asked.

"They're all in the display cabinet over there. Why don't you come and have a look?" The waitress held out her hand for Florence.

I decided I'd better go with them, in case Florence tried to choose the biggest cake in the cabinet.

What do you mean, like mother like daughter?

As we walked across the shop, the woman at the counter fixed us with her gaze. I thought if I introduced myself it might defrost her a little.

"Hi, I'm Jill Maxwell. That's my husband, Jack, over at the table, and this is our daughter, Florence. We live in the old watermill."

"Pleased to meet you, I'm sure. I'm Marcy Drinkwater. I'm the owner of this establishment."

"It's the first time we've been in here."

"How long have you lived in Middle Tweaking?"

"Just a couple of months."

"And this is your first visit to the tea room?"

"Err, yeah. Sorry." For reasons I can't explain, I felt as though I needed to justify myself. "We've been rather busy, as you can imagine."

"Hmm. I've been running this tea room for almost twenty-five years now. You won't find a better cup of tea or coffee in a twenty-mile radius."

"Right."

"Has Marian taken your order?"

"Yes, I have, Miss Drinkwater." The waitress sounded even more nervous. "The little girl is just deciding what bun she'd like."

Florence's eyes were as big as saucers, as she surveyed the cakes on offer. "Can I have that one please, Mummy?"

She pointed to a cake with icing and a small chocolate flake on top.

"The flake cake?"

"Yes, please."

"Okay. And Jack and I will have scones with jam and cream, please."

"Have you written all that down, Marian?" Marcy Drinkwater snapped.

"I'm just doing it now, Miss Drinkwater."

"Be quick about it. There are other people to serve, you know."

I glanced again around the shop, which was still empty.

"She's a bit much, isn't she?" Jack said in a whisper once we were back at the table.

"You're not kidding. I feel really sorry for that poor girl. Fancy having to work for that ogre."

Having the 'ogre' stare at us while we were eating was a little off-putting, but the tea was very good, and the scones were to die for.

"Did you enjoy your milkshake?" Jack asked Florence.

"It was yummy." She had a pink milk moustache.

"What about the bun?" I said. "You haven't eaten very much of it." She'd eaten the icing, the chocolate flake, and maybe a few crumbs of the cake itself.

"I'm full, Mummy."

Suddenly, Miss Drinkwater was standing next to our table. How had she got there? I hadn't seen her move.

"Is there something wrong with that cake, young lady?" she snapped.

I stepped in. "The cake is fine, Miss Drinkwater. Florence just isn't very hungry at the moment."

"Very well." She snatched the plate from the table,

huffing to herself all the way back to the counter.

We were just getting ready to leave when another couple, clearly tourists, came through the door. They'd no sooner stepped foot inside than Marian ushered them to a table and asked if they were ready to place their order.

"Is it just me?" Jack said, when we were back at the house. "Or is the woman who runs that tea room psycho?"

"There's no wonder the place is empty. I bet no one ever goes there twice."

***

Freda Pearldiver was a charming woman who couldn't do enough for me. After showing me into her gorgeous living room, she disappeared into the kitchen, and returned a few minutes later, carrying a silver tray with a pot of tea on it.

"I do hope you like loose tea, Jill?"

"To be perfectly honest with you, Freda, I can't remember the last time I had any."

"In that case, you're in for a real treat." She picked up the pot and poured a cup for me. "Do help yourself to milk and sugar."

I took a sip.

"What do you think?"

"It's lovely." I picked a couple of tea leaves off my tongue.

"I buy it from a small shop called Tea for Three."

"Right." I was trying not to choke on the tea leaves. "Don't you normally use a tea strainer with loose tea?"

"I find that spoils the taste. Now, you said you wanted

to talk to me about Maxine."

"Indirectly, yes. It's actually related to my daughter, Florence. I'm not sure if the headmistress mentioned it to you, but my husband, Jack, is a human."

"Yes, Miss Bogart told me."

"I understand that Maxine's father is a human too?"

"That's right, but Graham walked out on us not long after Maxine was born, so he hasn't played any part in her upbringing."

"That can't have been easy for you."

"It wasn't, particularly not at first, but it got easier as the years went by."

"We're trying to decide how much magic we should teach Florence."

"*We*?" Freda looked shocked. "Surely your husband doesn't know you and your daughter are sups?"

Oh bum!

"No, of course not. I meant to say that *I'm* trying to decide. I'd planned to teach her just a handful of spells for now, and then when she's older, I can introduce her to the more advanced spells. I'm curious to hear how you approached this with Maxine?"

"Actually, I didn't teach Maxine any magic at all until she was eleven years old. In fact, she didn't even know she was a witch until then."

"Really? That does surprise me."

"She only found out she was a witch when the invitation from CASS arrived. To be honest, I never for one moment expected her to be invited to attend CASS. It came as a total surprise."

"What happened when she found out that she was a witch?"

"At first, she simply didn't believe it. Then, she became very angry with me for keeping her in the dark."

"But she still wanted to go to CASS?"

"Once she'd calmed down, I gave her the choice. I said it was entirely up to her whether she went there or not."

"And how is she doing there?"

"It was very difficult for her at first because most of the kids live in the sup world. And, the few that do live in the human world have known they were sups all their lives. That's why I think my decision not to tell her was a mistake. Thankfully, she's settled in now and is doing well with all of her studies."

"That must be a relief for you."

"It is. What will you do if Florence gets an invitation to CASS? It's not like you can discuss it with your husband, is it?"

"I have no idea. Look, Freda, I'll be honest with you, the main reason I wanted to talk to you was to ask if you'd give me permission to speak with Maxine. I'd love to get her take on all of this, but I'll understand if you'd prefer I didn't."

"I have no objections, but I'll need to check with her first, to see if she's okay with it."

"Of course."

"I'll be speaking to her in the next couple of days, so I'll let you know what she says."

"That's great. Thanks."

"I'm curious about one thing, Jill. Don't you worry that Florence might say something to your husband? Tell him that she's a witch, I mean?"

"Every day, but Florence and I have regular chats about it, and I always make sure she knows it has to be our little secret."

Chapter 13

It was Monday morning and I was feeling rested after the weekend. On Saturday, after I'd got back from speaking to Freda Pearldiver, Jack, Florence and I had spent the rest of the day at home.

On Sunday, we'd taken a drive into the countryside for a picnic. The weather had been gorgeous, and Florence had been on her best behaviour. The only *dog* in the ointment had been the lazy Chihuahua. Apparently, Buddy was not fond of long walks. Or any kind of walk. We'd only been going for about ten minutes when he refused to budge. Jack had to carry him for most of the day, which was ironic after the way he'd complained to me about being manhandled. It's not like he's an old dog; he's barely more than a puppy. He's just bone idle.

I'd just set off for the office when a man, dressed in trainers, jeans and a red cardigan, stepped into the road and flagged me down. I'd seen him a few times around the village, but I'd never actually spoken to him.

I lowered the window. "Can I help you?"

"I'm sorry to catch you on your way out like this. I'm Rupert Schubert, the vicar of Tweaking parish. You're new to the village, aren't you?"

"Yeah, we moved into the old watermill a couple of months ago."

"I thought so. You have a little girl, don't you?"

"Florence, yes. I'm Jill and my husband's name is Jack."

"Jack and Jill, eh?" He grinned. "You must have a fairy tale marriage."

There were times when I seriously considered changing

my name by deed poll. There were only so many times you could hear people make the same few jokes. What name would I choose instead? Rosemary? Maybe Lucinda? Suggestions on a postcard to: No one cares, c/o the old watermill, Middle Tweaking.

Anyway, I digress. The man handed me a flyer.

"Freaking Tweaking? What's that?"

"It's the festival that's held on Tweaking Meadows every year. It's great fun. There are lots of rides and games for the kids, and plenty for the adults, too. I do hope that you and your family will be able to attend."

"We'll do our best." Not if I had anything to do with it. "Thanks very much."

"I'd better let you get going." He stepped back from the car. "It was nice to meet you, Jill."

"You too."

Once I was out of the village, I screwed up the leaflet and threw it onto the back seat.

***

As I walked towards my office building, I could hear an almighty racket coming from inside. It took me a few seconds to realise what it was.

Barking. Lots of barking.

The stairs were full of dogs and their owners. Dogs of every shape, size and breed, from a tiny Yorkshire terrier through to an enormous Irish wolfhound. They must be here for the free shampoo offer to promote the grand opening of Bubbles. It looked like Farah Close was going to have her work cut out.

Somehow, I had to try to negotiate my way up the

stairs.

"Excuse me. Excuse me, please. Can I get past? Excuse me."

As I fought my way up the stairs, the dogs began to bark even more; a couple of them even snapped at me. How I managed to squeeze past the St Bernard and its portly owner, I'll never know.

Phew! I'd made it to the office.

"Good morning, Mrs V."

"Morning, Jill. You managed to get past the dogs, then?"

"Barely."

"I had an awful time of it. A little Pekingese took a real dislike to me. I thought he was going to have my ankle. I do hope it isn't going to be like this every day. At least the clowns didn't bite."

"They're all here for the offer of a free shampoo at Bubbles. I'm sure it will ease up after today."

"I do hope so. Did you have a nice weekend?"

"Yes, thanks. We all went for a picnic in the countryside yesterday."

"How lovely. It was a beautiful day, wasn't it? Armi and I spent the afternoon sitting in the back garden, enjoying the fresh air."

"What about the squirrels? Didn't they cause you any problems?"

"I think we may have solved that particular issue."

"How did you manage that? Did you persuade the pest control people to take them away?"

"No. Armi came up with an ingenious idea. He bought two giant parasols, and we sat underneath those. Apart from the sound of the acorns pounding on the parasol, it was quite delightful."

There was no sign of Winky in my office, but Agents Ricardo and Lulu had moved the sofa next to the window and were keeping watch on the building opposite.

"Anything happening over there?" I said.

"Not yet."

"Where's Winky?"

"He had to nip out. I don't suppose there's any chance of some food, is there? This surveillance is hungry work."

"Of course. Is salmon okay again?"

"That would be lovely." Lulu licked her lips.

I'd just finished putting out the salmon when Bertie the pigeon appeared on the ledge outside the open window. Fortunately, the two undercover police cats were too busy eating to notice him.

"Good morning, Jill." The pigeon waved a wing at me.

"Morning, Bertie. How are you?"

"Excellent. It's a beautiful day. Why do you spend all your time in this stuffy office?"

"It's not through choice, trust me, but I have to earn a living somehow."

Harold and Ida had lived on the ledge until two years ago when they'd decided to retire to the coast. The last I heard they were living in Southend. About six months ago, Bertie and his brother, Bobby, had moved onto the ledge. They were both big birds, and I really do mean *big*.

"It's slim pickings out there today," Bertie said. "Bobby and I have been scratching around on the ground near the benches for the best part of two hours, and we barely picked up a couple of crumbs between us."

"Oh dear. I'm sorry to hear that. Where is Bobby?"

"Having a nap. All that pecking has worn him out. He doesn't have my levels of stamina. Did I ever tell you that I used to be a racer, Jill?"

"A racing *pigeon*?"

"No, a racing *zebra*." He laughed. "Of course, a racing pigeon."

"Did you take part in any competitions?"

"Yes, both Bobby and I did. I was much faster than him, as you'd expect. As a matter of fact, I was crowned Washbridge's Fastest Pigeon of The Year two years running."

"That's very impressive."

"There was a lot less of me back then."

There must have been.

Mrs V came into my office. "What are they doing in here?" She gestured towards the cats.

"It's okay, they're just undercover—" Oh bum! When would I ever learn to engage my brain before speaking?

"Undercover?"

"They—err—sneaked in here *under cover* of darkness."

"Why didn't you just throw them out?"

"I—err—I'm going to, but they looked so hungry that I thought the least I could do was to give them some food first."

"You're too soft. That's your trouble."

"You're right. Did you come in to tell me something?"

"Just that I forgot to tell you Mr Edwards rang before you arrived. He wondered if there'd been any progress on his case. I said you'd call him back."

"Right. Leave it with me."

I'd been dreading this moment. What exactly was I supposed to tell Rusty? That he really had lost his marbles? I couldn't do that. Not yet, anyway. I owed it to him to have at least one more crack at his case.

***

I couldn't just turn up on the doorstep of the house where the alleged shooting had taken place and tell them I was a private investigator. Once they knew I was working for the guy across the park, who insisted he'd seen someone being shot in their house, they'd turn me away for sure. If I was going to get inside, I'd need to use magic, or come up with a cunning plan.

Fortunately, as you're no doubt already aware, plans of the cunning variety are my speciality.

It's not everyone who can carry off a uniform, but I look really good in them — even if I do say so myself.

The middle-aged man who answered the door was holding a golf putter.

"There's a sticker on the dashboard," he said. "Didn't you see it?"

"Sorry?" I hadn't the faintest idea what he meant.

"My resident's sticker is plainly on display. I'm Mr Smart."

"I'm sorry. I don't know what you're talking about."

He looked me up and down. "You are the parking warden, aren't you?"

"No."

"You look like one. Are you sure?"

"I'm positive. I'm from the fire service."

He poked his head out of the door and looked left and right. "Is there a fire somewhere?"

"No, it's nothing like that. I'm from the prevention division of the fire service. I'm calling on all the houses in the street to do a spot check, just to make sure everything is in order."

"Did you let us know you were coming?"

"No. The whole point of these checks is to drop in unannounced."

"I see. I suppose you'd better come in, then. What's your name?"

"Rhona — err — Burns."

"*Burns!*" He laughed. "That's rather an unfortunate name, given your occupation, isn't it? Don't trip over the putting mat." He pointed to a strip of green matting which looked just like a crazy golf hole. "Do you play golf, Rhona?"

"Me? Err, no. Is it alright to take a look around the house?"

"Help yourself."

A woman appeared in the doorway at the other end of the hallway.

"What's going on, Jeffrey? Have you told her that we have a resident's parking permit?"

"She isn't the parking warden, Deirdre. She's from the fire prevention service."

"She looks like a parking warden."

"I'm not," I reassured her. "My name is Rhona Burns, and, as your husband said, I work for the fire prevention service."

"Did you hear that, Deirdre?" The man laughed. "Her

name is *Burns*?"

"Of course I heard her. I'm not deaf."

"But it's *Burns,* and she works for the fire prevention service. Do you get it?"

The woman continued to stare at me, stony-faced. "What do you want?"

"I'm checking on all the properties in the street. It shouldn't take more than thirty minutes or so. Is it alright if I make a start?"

"I suppose so, but please be quick."

The question now was what exactly did a fire prevention officer do? I'd brought a clipboard and notepad with me, so I began to make meaningless notes as I walked around. I started in the kitchen and took a close look at the various appliances, tapping each one, and then scribbling on the notepad.

I was just about to leave the kitchen when the woman said, "What about the smoke alarm? Shouldn't you have checked that?"

Oh bum. I had no idea how to test one of those.

"Err, actually, no. This particular inspection doesn't include the smoke alarms. We have a separate unit that deals with those."

I hurried out of the kitchen before she could ask any more awkward questions. After spending a few minutes in the lounge, I headed upstairs. The room in which Rusty had supposedly seen the shooting incident turned out to be the master bedroom. I looked high and low, but I could see nothing to suggest someone had been shot in that room. There were no bullet holes or blood. Or bodies. I looked across the park at Rusty's house; had he really witnessed a shooting in this room? It was looking less and less likely.

I came out of the master bedroom and was about to make a quick 'check' on the other rooms when I heard the man and woman going at it like cat and dog downstairs.

"What was I supposed to do?" the man said. "Turn her away?"

"You should have told her to make an appointment."

"But she said it's supposed to be a random check."

"That's your trouble, Jeffrey. You're weak. You let everyone walk all over you."

"Just a minute, Deirdre, that's not—"

"Go back to your stupid golf. That's all you care about, isn't it?"

The argument continued in that vein for the next few minutes, with the woman throwing more and more vicious insults at her husband. The poor man tried to defend himself, but he was no match for her acerbic tongue.

When they eventually relented, I made my way back downstairs. There was no sign of the woman, but the man had gone back to his putting.

"Thanks very much," I said. "Everything seems to be in order. You have a clean bill of health."

"Excellent."

"I can see myself out."

Chapter 14

I was about to interview Mrs Jones, the cook at Tweaking Manor. I didn't need to take the car because she lived in Middle Tweaking. Her house was two doors down from where Walter Staniforth had once lived. Just prior to his retirement, Staniforth had been the lead detective on a case involving the murder, by poisoning, of a young woman. In his determination to solve the case and retire on a high, Staniforth had framed an innocent young man called Arnold Kramer. Fortunately, I'd been able to find the real murderer, which had resulted in Arnold Kramer's release. When the truth had come out, Staniforth had been arrested and subsequently jailed. His house was now occupied by a couple with a young boy about the same age as Florence.

Mrs Jones answered the door wearing a pair of green rubber gloves.

"Is it that time already?" She checked her watch. "I'm really sorry. I've been cleaning the oven and I totally lost track of time. I've been meaning to do it for weeks now. I hate that job, don't you?"

"Yes, it's horrible." Not that I'd ever done it. "I do appreciate you sparing me the time, Mrs Jones."

"No problem, and please call me Lydia. Do come in. My husband has just gone into Washbridge, so we'll have the house to ourselves." Just me and Mrs Jones, then. "I'll just take these gloves off and then I'm all yours. Why don't you go through to the lounge and I'll be with you in two ticks?"

The room was fussy, much like Mrs Jones. Every surface

was covered with ornaments, all in the shape of weird fish-lizard like creatures. I took a seat on the sofa next to the window and a few minutes later, Mrs Jones joined me.

"I was just admiring your ornaments, Lydia."

"As you've probably guessed, I'm a big fan of the axolotl."

"Axo—?"

"Lotl. They're so cute, don't you think?"

"They're lovely." If you like fish with legs.

"I believe you want to talk to me about the missing goblet."

"That's right. How long have you worked for Caroline?"

"On and off, it must be nearly fifteen years now."

"*On and off?*"

"I did leave for a short time a few years ago."

"May I ask why?"

"It was that husband of hers. He was a difficult man to work for, very rude with a terrible short temper. On that particular day, the crust on the pie wasn't to his liking, and he snapped at me for the umpteenth time. I'm sorry to say that I lost my temper and turned on him. He sacked me on the spot."

"How long was it before you went back there?"

"Just over a couple of months. Caroline came to the house and practically begged me to go back. I wasn't sure if I should or not, but Caroline said that she'd warned her husband that if he ever spoke to me like that again, she'd kick him out. Caroline is quiet most of the time, but when she gets riled, you know about it."

"The house and family seem to have fallen on hard times."

"That's an understatement. The manor used to be such a happy, lively place. It's hard to imagine now, but it was once a warm, welcoming house. Now, it's just a pale shadow of its former self. It's Caroline that I feel sorry for. She's doing her best to turn things around, but she's been landed with a huge tax bill. I'm not sure even she will be able to pull anything out of the bag this time. To be honest, I fully expect to be out of a job soon."

"How well do you know the other members of the family, Lydia?"

"Some of them better than others. Elizabeth is a lovely woman. She's always polite and she treats everyone with respect. Her brother is a different kettle of fish altogether."

"Ransom?"

"Yes. That man is a horror. He always was, and he probably always will be. I heard the two of them arguing on that night."

"On the night the goblet went missing?"

"Yes. I'd just finished for the day and I was on my way out of the kitchen when I heard them going at it in the hallway. I hung back a while because I didn't want to walk into the middle of it."

"Could you hear what they were saying?"

"No, and to be honest, I wasn't interested. I just wanted to get home. As soon as they'd finished, I left the house."

"Do you have any idea who might have taken the goblet?"

"None. I'm sure the others must have already told you this, but it's an ugly thing. Caroline only kept it on display because of its important place in the family's history, and I know she was devastated when she discovered it had gone missing."

"Mulgrave told me that there used to be more staff at the manor house."

"That's right. At its peak, there were six of us. Now it's just me and Mulgrave, and I'm surprised he's still there."

"Why do you say that?"

"Caroline was forced to cut his wages by almost half."

"That's a big drop."

"I know. I fully expected him to leave. With his experience, he could easily have walked into a similar job elsewhere. There's a shortage of experienced butlers in this country. I guess he stayed out of a sense of loyalty to Caroline."

***

I'd just left Mrs Jones' house and was making my way back to the old watermill, when I heard someone calling to me, "Hey there!"

I turned around to find the werewolf girl's mother running down the road. By the time she'd caught up with me, she was red in the face and out of breath.

"Thanks for waiting." She wheezed. "I'm not as fit as I used to be. I just wanted to introduce myself. I'm Donna. Donna Poulsen."

"Pleased to meet you. Jill Maxwell."

"I thought about coming over to say hello on Saturday at the dance class, but I figured it might be better to do it when your husband wasn't around. For obvious reasons."

"Are you sure you're okay?"

"Yeah, but I could do with a sit down. Are you in a hurry, Jill?"

"Not particularly."

"How about we go in there and grab a cup of tea?" She pointed to Tweaking Tea Rooms.

"Have you been in there before, Donna?"

"No, what's it like?"

"The tea is okay, but the owner's a bit — err — much."

"I'm still up for it if you are."

"Sure. Why not?"

As soon as we walked through the door, a waitress came scurrying over. It wasn't Marian, but this young girl was obviously working under the same orders.

"Welcome to Tweaking Tea Rooms," she gabbled. "We have a free window table at the moment if you'd like it."

I glanced around and, once again, the tea room was deserted, except of course for Miss Drinkwater who was sitting guard by the counter.

"I'll just have a cup of tea, please," I said.

"Same for me." Donna nodded.

The waitress looked relieved that we'd ordered so promptly.

"Is that the owner?" Donna whispered. "Over by the counter?"

"Yeah, that's her. Miss Drinkwater. She terrorises these poor waitresses."

A couple of minutes later, our tea arrived, and Donna began to fill me in on her background. She worked as a midwife and her husband was an engineer.

"I have to say, Jill, it's nice to know there's another sup in the village. Ronnie and I were beginning to wonder if we'd made a mistake by moving here."

"Where did you used to live?"

"In an apartment in Washbridge. We thought village life would be better for Wendy, but it came as something of a surprise when we got here, and discovered we were the only sups. By the way, I don't know if Florence mentioned it, but Wendy would love for her to come over to our house to play some time."

"That would be lovely. And Wendy is more than welcome to come to ours. Does she like dogs?"

"Wendy? She loves them. What kind do you have?"

"A Chihuahua named Buddy. We've only had him for a few days. Florence told me that Wendy has a rat?"

"She does. Ratty. He's a lovely little thing. Very friendly."

"I hope you don't mind me asking this, Donna, but does Wendy know she's a werewolf?"

"Of course. It's not really something you can hide."

"I guess not."

"We always take her back to Candlefield during the full moon. What about Florence? Does she know she's a witch?"

"Yes, she does."

"That must be very difficult. With your husband being a human, I mean?"

"It can be."

We chatted for another twenty minutes and we were just about to leave when my phone buzzed. When I saw who it was, I cancelled the call.

"Just my new accountant." I rolled my eyes. "She and I didn't really hit it off. I'm going to have to find a new one."

"Have you considered using Mr Bacus?"

"Who's he?"

"I can't vouch for his work, but he's a nice old guy. We've met him a few times in the pub."

"Is he local, then?"

"Yes. He lives somewhere near the church, I believe. It might be worth talking to him."

"Thanks, Donna. I might just do that."

***

Jack must have spotted me through the window because even before I reached the gate, both he and Florence appeared in the doorway. Florence came running down the path and threw herself into my arms.

"Mummy! Why is Buddy so slow?" She demanded to know.

"Because he's only a tiny dog with short legs."

"My friend, Andrew, has a small dog called Rum. Andrew says Rum runs really fast after the ball when he throws it. Why won't Buddy? He just walks really slowly."

"Would you like me to have another word with him? Maybe, I can give him some tips to make him go faster?"

"Yes, please."

"Anyway, darling, did you have a nice day at school?"

"Yes. Miss Soap asked if Daddy was going to pick me up today."

"Did she really?" I glanced over at Jack. "That was very nice of her, wasn't it?" I picked Florence up and carried her to the door. "Florence tells me that her teacher was asking after you today."

"Was she?" He shrugged, nonchalantly.

"Can I go and play with my dolls' house, Mummy?"

"Of course you can, darling." I put her down, and she ran into the house and up the stairs.

"So, Jack, how was Miss Hope?"

"Same as usual. She told me that Florence had been a good girl and she'd been working very hard."

"Did she tell you that she'd missed you the other day?"

"You're not jealous, are you?"

"Of course not. I know you'd never look at another woman when you have me."

"Because you're so beautiful and smart, I suppose?"

"Obviously there's that, but also because I'd turn you into a cockroach if you did. Anyway, I've just been talking to Wendy's mum."

"Is Wendy the big girl from the dance class?"

"Yeah. Her mum's name is Donna. She seems really nice."

"What did she have to say?"

"That she was glad they weren't the only sups in the village."

"She's a sup?"

"Yeah. The whole family are werewolves."

"You didn't mention it on Saturday."

"Sorry, I intended to, but I forgot all about it. She and I have just been for a cup of tea in the tea room."

"Tweaking Tea Rooms? Whatever possessed you to go back there?"

"It wasn't my idea. Donna said she fancied a drink."

"Was the ogre on duty?"

"Yes, and we got the icy stare treatment. Apparently, Donna and her husband used to live in Washbridge city centre. She asked if Florence could go over to their house to play sometime. I said she could, and that Wendy was welcome to come over here too."

"That'll be nice for Florence."

"I'm starving. How long's dinner?"

"Another twenty minutes."

"Right. While you're seeing to that, I'll have a word with that Chihuahua. Where is Buddy?"

"He's out in the back garden."

"Hey, you!" I shouted at the dozing dog.

"Do you mind?" He glanced up. "I was fast asleep."

"Tough. I thought you and I had struck a deal."

"We did. I've been playing with the little squirt, haven't I?"

"Less of the little squirt. Her name is Florence. You need to show more enthusiasm. When she throws the ball, you're supposed to run after it, grab it, and then run back again."

"Why? What's the hurry? I get the job done, don't I?"

"If you want to carry on eating your expensive food, you'd better buck your ideas up. Otherwise, it's back to the slop for you."

"You drive a hard bargain, lady."

That evening, it was my turn to take Florence to bed. By the time I was halfway through the second reading of her favourite book, she'd fallen asleep, so I crept out of the room and down the stairs.

"I could kill a cuppa, Jack."

"Me too." He looked up from the book he was reading. "You know where the kettle is."

"I bet you'd make a cup of tea if Miss Soap wanted one."

Chapter 15

The next morning when I left the house, Florence didn't see me off at the door because she was in the garden, playing with Buddy. The dog was dashing up and down the lawn like greased lightning. My threat to bring back the 'slop' had clearly done the trick.

I was just about to get into the car when my phone rang; it was Freda Pearldiver.

"Jill, I hope I haven't called too early, but I wanted to catch you before I went to work."

"No problem. I was just on my way out."

"I spoke to Maxine yesterday and mentioned that you'd like to talk to her. She said she'd be happy to meet with you. In fact, it sounds like she's something of a fangirl. Apparently, she has your picture stuck to the inside of her locker."

"That's a little embarrassing. Still, I'm glad she's agreed to talk to me. When do you think that could be arranged, Freda?"

"She can meet with you tomorrow afternoon if that works for you. Maxine has a free period at two o'clock."

"That's great. I'll pop over then. Will you let her know?"

"I will."

"Thanks again, Freda."

That was great news. I was eager to hear how Maxine felt about not knowing she was a witch until she was eleven years old. Maybe that would help me to come to a decision regarding Florence's future.

***

I'd just parked the car in Washbridge when my phone rang again. It was Pearl, who sounded frantic.

"Pearl, slow down. I can't tell what you're saying."

"I've just called Mum, and something's not right."

"What do you mean, not right?"

"She sounded like she was trying not to cry. I asked her what was wrong, and she said it was nothing, but I'm worried. I can't get away from the shop because I'm the only one here. I've tried calling Amber, but she isn't picking up, as per usual. I don't suppose you could pop over there and see what's going on, could you?"

"Sure. I'll go straight over there now."

"Call me back and let me know what's happening, won't you?"

"Of course. I'll phone you as soon as I know, but don't worry. I'm sure it's nothing."

I made sure no one was around, and then magicked myself over to Aunt Lucy's house. There was no answer when I knocked on the door, so I let myself in.

"Aunt Lucy? Aunt Lucy? It's Jill!"

There was no sign of her, but Barry came charging down the stairs and nearly knocked me over.

"Not now, Barry. I'm looking for Aunt Lucy. Do you know where she is?"

"She isn't here."

"I can see that."

"Maybe she's gone for a walk. Lucy loves walks."

"Hmm. Let's try the garden."

I hurried through the house and out of the back door. Aunt Lucy was standing next to the wall, in tears. She was being consoled by her neighbour, Charlie Roundtree.

Barry, who was much quicker than me, dashed over to her, jumped up and began to lick her face.

"I'm alright, Barry." She pushed him down gently.

"What's wrong, Aunt Lucy?" I took her hand. "Pearl called me."

"It's nothing, honestly. Pearl shouldn't have bothered you."

"It's no bother, but I do want to know what's going on."

"I'm just being silly."

"She's not being silly at all," Charlie said. "Lucy's upset, and she has every right to be. Take a look over there." He pointed to the far side of the garden.

I'd been so focussed on Aunt Lucy that I hadn't noticed the flower bed near the gate. Most of the flowers had been pulled up by their roots and thrown everywhere. The rest of them had been trampled underfoot. It was a disaster area.

"What happened?"

"Vandals did it," Aunt Lucy said through her tears. "They came in the early hours of the morning."

"Did you see them?"

"I didn't, but Charlie did. Didn't you, Charlie?"

He nodded. "I was in bed and I thought I heard a noise. When I looked out of the window, I could see them, trampling all over the flower bed, laughing their heads off. When I shouted, they ran away like the cowards they are. I should have gone downstairs and tackled them."

"I'm glad you didn't," Aunt Lucy said. "Who knows what people like that are capable of?"

"Did you get a good look at them?" I asked.

"I'm afraid not. It was barely light; they were just shadows."

"I really thought I had a chance of winning the competition." Aunt Lucy sobbed. "I've spent so many hours on this garden."

"Come on." I put my arm around her. "Let's go inside."

"Is there anything more I can do?" Charlie asked.

"No, thanks. I've got this now."

Once she was seated in the lounge, I went through to the kitchen to make her a cup of tea.

"Is Lucy alright?" Barry said.

"She will be when she's had a drink."

"Do you think she'd like one of my bones?"

"That's very thoughtful of you, but I don't think that will be necessary."

By the time I took the tea through, Aunt Lucy had managed to compose herself.

"Thanks, Jill. I'm sorry you had to come over. I'm just being a silly old woman."

"No, you're not. It must have been an awful shock. I'd better call Pearl to let her know you're alright. She'll be worried."

After I'd updated Pearl, I sat with Aunt Lucy until I was satisfied that she was okay.

If I ever got my hands on those vandals, they'd be sorry.

***

When I walked into the outer office, I did a double take because sitting on Mrs V's desk was a little white poodle.

"Good morning, Jill."

"Morning. Who's your little friend?"

"I thought I'd call her Polly. The name suits her, don't you think?"

"Where did she come from?"

"When I got back from the loo earlier, this little lady was waiting outside the office door for me. Armi and I have been talking about getting a dog for some time now, and then fate delivers Polly to me. It's a miracle."

"Maybe, but there is another more obvious explanation."

"What's that, dear?"

"Do you think it's possible that Polly came from down the corridor? From Bubbles?"

"I wouldn't have thought so."

"You don't think it's something of a coincidence that a dog grooming parlour opened next door yesterday, and today a poodle turned up outside our door?"

"Hmm. I suppose it's possible."

"Why don't I take a walk down to Bubbles, to see if they're missing a poodle?"

"If you like, but I'm sure that's not where Polly came from."

The young woman in reception at the grooming parlour had clearly been chosen for her bubbliness.

"Good morning. Welcome to Bubbles," she gushed. "Do you have an appointment?" She leaned forward. "Have you left your dog outside?"

"Actually, I'm not here to get my dog groomed. I was just wondering if you'd lost a poodle."

"A poodle? I wouldn't have thought so."

"I work in the office just down the corridor, and we seem to have acquired one. A little white one."

"We do have a white poodle waiting to be clipped, but I'm sure I fastened her in the cage."

"It might be worth checking, don't you think?"

"I won't be a minute." She disappeared through the door behind her, and returned a couple of minutes later, looking panic-stricken. "I could have sworn I locked it. Is Miranda okay?"

Miranda?

"Yes, she's fine. She's with my receptionist. Why don't you come with me and get her?"

"I will, thanks. You won't say anything about this to my boss, will you? I only started here yesterday, and I don't want to lose this job."

"I won't say a word, but you really must be more careful in future. The dog could have gone down the stairs, out through the main door, and into the street."

"I know. I feel terrible. I don't know what I was thinking."

"Come on, then. Let's go and get her." I led the way down the corridor.

"My name's Delilah, by the way."

"My, my, what a nice name."

When the two of us walked into the outer office, Mrs V's face fell.

"This is Delilah, Mrs V. She works at Bubbles, and it seems they're missing a poodle called Miranda."

"*Miranda?*" Mrs V shook her head. "That name doesn't suit Polly at all."

"Who's Polly?" Delilah said.

"That's the name Mrs V gave to the poodle."

"Her name's definitely Miranda. She's waiting for a clip. Is it okay if I take her?"

For a moment, I thought Mrs V might grab the poodle and make a break for it, but reluctantly she handed her to

Delilah.

"Thank you. Both of you. And thanks for not saying anything to my boss. I really need this job because my fiancé, Sam, and I are getting married next year."

"Just make sure you double-check the cages in future."

"Don't worry. I will."

After Delilah and the poodle had left, Mrs V looked crestfallen.

"I'm sorry, Mrs V, but you couldn't keep Polly—err— Miranda. Think how devastated her owner would have been if they'd come to pick her up, only to find that she was missing."

"You're right, dear. I know you are. But I think this is a sign that we should have a dog. A little poodle just like Polly."

While Mrs V was poodle dreaming, I slipped into my office.

"Good morning, Winky. Good morning, Ricardo. Good morning, Lulu. Anything to report?"

"Plenty, but we aren't at liberty to share it with you, I'm afraid." Officer Lulu jumped down from the windowsill and onto my desk.

"We're all rather hungry, Jill," Winky said.

"Oh? It's a bit early, isn't it?"

"It's never too early for salmon."

"I do have to go out in a few minutes, so I suppose I might as well feed you now."

Once I'd given them the salmon, I went over to my desk to check the post. All bills, as usual. I was just about to leave when I remembered what Donna had told me about the accountant who lived in the village, so I took the receipts and invoices from the bottom drawer of my desk and shoved them in a carrier bag. I figured I could show him what I had, to see if he could work with that.

"Right, Winky. I'm off now. Goodbye, Agents Lulu and Ricardo."

***

I suspected I knew who was behind the recent spate of bank robberies, but to test my theory, and to help me track him down, I needed to speak to the man who'd held us hostage in Coffee Animal. The only way I'd managed to get an interview with him had been to use the 'doppelganger' spell in order to pose as his solicitor.

The bank robber, whose name was Darren Black, was seated in the interview room, with one foot up on the table.

"What's up, man?" he said, through a mouthful of gum. "Any chance of getting me out of here?"

"No chance whatsoever, Darren."

"What am I paying you for, then?"

"*You* aren't paying me. The government is. And there's no way an armed bank robber is going to be allowed out on bail, so you can forget about that."

"What are you doing here, then?"

"I may have a way for you to get your sentence reduced."

"Hold on." He sat up. "I've not been found guilty yet."

"Come on, Darren, let's get real. They've got you on CCTV in the bank with a gun in your hand. And then there are all the witnesses in the coffee shop. Your only chance is to plead guilty and do whatever it takes to get a reduced sentence."

"Like what?"

"Give up the identity of your accomplice."

"You want me to be a snitch?" He scoffed. "No way Darren Black is going to grass on anyone."

"That's all very admirable, Darren. Honour among thieves and all that. But the man you're protecting left you to carry the can."

"That's just the way things played out. It wasn't his fault."

"Are you really that naive?"

"The getaway car was supposed to be on the street at the side of the bank, but it wasn't there. That's why I made a break for the coffee shop."

"And where was your accomplice when all this was happening?"

"He was behind me when we left the bank, but then I just kind of lost him. I don't know where he went."

"There never was a getaway car, Darren. Your accomplice's plan was always to leave you to face the music while he got away with the money."

"Says you."

"This isn't the first time he's done this. He has a track record of doing exactly the same thing, time after time. He uses mugs like you to —"

"Hang on. Who are you calling a *mug*?"

"Think about it for a minute. You're in prison while he's walking around with a bag full of money. In my book, that makes you the mug. As I was saying, he's done this several times before. He finds himself a partner, they carry out the job together, and he gets away, scot-free, leaving his partner-in-crime to carry the can."

"If that's true, I'll kill him."

"It is true, but you aren't going to get the chance to kill him. By the time you get out, you'll be too old and frail to hurt anyone. Unless you wise up and tell me who he is, and where I can find him."

"I don't know his real name; he just called himself Romeo. And how am I supposed to know where he is if the police can't find him?"

"Is this the guy?" I handed him the photo that Daze had given me.

Even before he answered, I saw the recognition in his face. "Where did you get this photo from?"

"Never mind that. Is it the guy?"

"Yeah, that's Romeo."

"What can you tell me about him?"

"Nothing much. He first approached me in the Gardeners' Arms. He obviously knew about my record because he asked if I'd be interested in us doing a bank job together. I was a bit suspicious of him at first; I thought he might be the Old Bill. I told him no, but he kept coming back. In the end, he convinced me that it would be worth my while."

"Did you ever go to his place?"

"No, I have no idea where he lives. We always met in pubs while we were planning the job."

"What else can you tell me about him?"

"Not much really, except that—err—it's probably not important."

"What were you going to say?"

"It's just that, every time I met him, he was with a different woman. The guy's not bad looking, as you can see from his photograph, but he's nothing special."

"Do you know the women's names?"

"No. As soon as I turned up, he sent them packing so that we could talk business. One day, I asked him how he kept pulling all these birds. Turns out, he used some kind of dating agency."

"An app, you mean?"

"No, I don't think so. It was some place in Washbridge, I reckon."

Chapter 16

My visit to see Darren Black had certainly given me food for thought. Speaking of food, I was feeling rather peckish, and I knew exactly what would hit the mark. No, not a blueberry muffin. What I really fancied was a cupcake, so I magicked myself over to Cuppy C where Pearl was behind the counter.

"Thanks for checking on Mum, Jill. I can't believe what those vandals did to her garden. What kind of person would do something like that?"

"I don't know, but if I find out who it was, they'll be sorry." I glanced down at the display of cakes. "I'm not sure whether to have a strawberry or a lemon cupcake."

"Come on, Jill, it really shouldn't be that difficult to decide."

"Stop pressuring me. These things can't be rushed. Okay, I'll take the lemon. No, the strawberry."

"Are you sure?"

"Positive."

I'd just paid for my cupcake and coffee when I heard someone crying. Sitting at a table, at the far side of the room, were five elves, two of whom were in tears. The other three looked upset too, but it was none of my business.

I was just about to take a seat by the window when one of the elves spotted me.

"Excuse me!" he shouted. "Aren't you Jill Maxwell?"

"Yes, I am."

"She might be able to help us," he said to the others around the table. "I've heard she's brilliant."

Which of course was absolutely true.

"Help you how?"

"Would you come and join us? Please."

"Sure." I took a seat at the table next to theirs. "What's wrong?"

"Some of our friends have gone missing," said the elf who had called me over.

"*Some*? More than one?"

"Yes. We've all lost at least one friend."

"I've lost two," one of the two female elves said. "Jodie and Birdie. They've both gone missing."

"When exactly did this happen?"

"They all disappeared within the last couple of weeks. And it isn't just *our* friends. Lots of elves have disappeared and no one has any idea where they've gone."

"That's terrible," I said. "It may be totally unrelated, but when I was in here the other day, I was talking to Daze and Blaze, the rogue retrievers. Do you know them?"

"Of course. Everyone knows Daze."

"While I was talking to her, she got a call, telling her to go straight into the office. She mentioned something about missing persons."

"This has been all over The Candle newspaper for the last week or so," another of the elves chimed in. "I'm surprised you haven't seen it."

"I rarely get the chance to read the papers. Where did your friends go missing from?"

"Birdie and Jodie had been playing badminton at the sports centre, but they never made it home."

Another one of the elves piped up, "My friend had been swimming there. That was the last anyone saw of her."

"Did they all go missing from the sports centre?"

"My friend didn't," the other female elf said. "She'd been to the library."

"But isn't that next door to the sports centre?"

"Yes. Do you think you can help us, Jill?"

"I can try. I should probably speak to Daze first, to see where she's up to on this."

As soon as I left Cuppy C, I gave Daze a call, but it went straight to her voicemail, so I left a message, asking her to get back to me.

***

I really wasn't looking forward to this, but there was no point in putting it off any longer. Despite my best efforts, I'd been unable to find any evidence that the shooting incident, which Rusty claimed to have witnessed, had actually taken place.

The neighbours on either side of the house in question had seen and heard nothing. And when I'd looked around the master bedroom of the property in question, there had been no sign of a shooting, let alone a murder. The only thing of any note in the Smart household had been the obvious animosity between Mr and Mrs Smart. The blazing row they'd had while I'd been upstairs had been quite shocking. But having an argument was one thing, murder quite another. The fact that Mr Smart was alive and well, and able to argue with his wife, made a mockery of Rusty's claim that he'd been murdered.

I didn't want to hurt Rusty's feelings any more than I had to, so I'd suggested we meet at the park. I was hoping that a walk in the fresh air might soften the blow somewhat. He was waiting for me by the park gates. As soon as he spotted me, he gave me an enthusiastic wave, which made the task ahead even more daunting.

"This was a good idea of yours, Jill. I spend a lot of time looking out at the park, but not nearly enough time in it."

"It's a lovely day for it." We started down the path that cut through the park, towards the houses where the alleged incident had taken place.

"I'm very excited to hear what you have to tell me," Rusty said.

"I'm afraid it isn't good news. I've spent some considerable time investigating this matter, but I've drawn a complete blank. I've spoken to the neighbours on either side of the property in question, but they saw and heard nothing."

"Maybe she used a silencer, Jill. Have you thought of that?"

"I suppose it's possible, but there's more. I've been inside the property itself."

"How did you manage that?"

"We private investigators have our methods. I managed to get a good look around the house, and I spent a lot of time in the master bedroom, which is the room where you thought you saw the shooting. I have to tell you, Rusty, I've been at many crime scenes and there's always some trace of evidence left behind, but there was nothing to see in there. No signs of gunshots, no blood, nothing at all to suggest a shooting had taken place. And the fact is, Mr Smart is alive and well, and shows no sign of being injured."

"I just don't understand it, Jill." Rusty was clearly disappointed by my news. "I know what I saw."

We had almost reached the other side of the park when

I happened to look up. Coming through the gates, only a hundred yards ahead of us, were Mr and Mrs Smart.

Oh bum!

"Rusty, I think it might be best if we headed back now."

"But why, Jill? I'm disappointed by your news, but I'm enjoying our little walk. And your company of course."

"Mr and Mrs Smart, the couple from the property where you thought you saw the shooting, have just walked through that gate, and I don't really want them to see me."

He glanced over at the couple. "That's him! That's the man I saw being shot."

"He looks perfectly healthy, wouldn't you say?"

"Yes. I don't understand it."

"Come on, Rusty, let's go."

"That's not her."

"Sorry?"

"The woman with him. That isn't the woman I saw doing the shooting."

I managed to persuade Rusty that we should go back to his house. When I left him, he was still adamant that the woman he'd seen in the park with Mr Smart was not the same woman he'd seen shooting a man. By now, though, I was having serious doubts about Rusty's reliability as a witness. Even though I could have made a pretty penny by continuing with the case, I didn't want to take advantage of a man who was clearly delusional, so I'd told him I was sorry, but there was nothing more I could do. Although he was clearly disappointed, he had been very gracious, and thanked me for the work I'd done.

***

I'd tried without success to find a phone number for Mr Bacus, the accountant who lived in Middle Tweaking. Weirdly, he didn't seem to be listed anywhere online, or even in the local phone book. Never one to give up easily, I decided to kill two birds with one stone by calling in at the local store. I was sure that the Stock sisters would know where Mr Bacus lived. While I was there, I would pick up a couple of packets of custard creams if the new stock had arrived.

The woman behind the counter wasn't Cynthia Stock, but there was an obvious family resemblance, so I assumed she must be her sister, Marjorie. I knew, from my previous visit, that the custard creams were kept near to the carrots and tea bags. Unfortunately, when I got to that aisle, I discovered all of the stock had been moved around. Instead of carrots and tea bags there were now rubber gloves and Pot Noodles. Needless to say, there was no sign of the custard creams.

Thoroughly defeated, I went over to the counter.

"Hello." The woman looked up from what she was doing. "Are you new to the village?"

"No, we live in the old watermill."

"Ah, yes. My sister mentioned you. Welcome to Middle Tweaking."

"Thanks. I just popped in on the off chance that you might have restocked with custard creams."

"You're in luck. We had a delivery just this morning."

"Great. Where are they?"

"Now, where did we put them?" From under the counter, she brought out the large ledger that I'd seen her sister using. "Custard creams?" She flicked slowly through the pages. A couple of minutes later, she tapped one of the pages with her finger. "Here we are. If you turn around, you'll find them in the aisle on the far left. Halfway down on your right, next to the cat food."

"The cat food?"

"That's right. You can't miss them. They're in between the cat food and the Marmite."

"Right." I followed her directions, and sure enough, there were the custard creams. I figured I might never find them again, so I grabbed five packets instead of two.

"My, you certainly like your custard creams."

"I do, but then they are the king of biscuits."

"I'm rather partial to a Jammie Dodger myself."

"While I'm here, might I ask you for some information?"

"Of course. I'll help if I can."

"I've been told there's an accountant who lives in the village. A Mr Bacus?"

"Arthur? Yes, we use him ourselves. He's very good."

"Could you possibly tell me where he lives? I've looked for his phone number, but I couldn't find it anywhere."

"He lives in one of the cottages behind the church. Number thirty-two. He's almost always in."

"Thanks very much."

Mr Bacus' cottage was a quaint little place, spoiled only by the overgrown garden. I rang the doorbell and a few moments later, the door creaked open and a face peered out of the gap.

"Can I help you, young lady?"

Mr Bacus looked seventy if he was a day. He was

wearing trousers which were an inch too short, and a green cardigan. Clearly the man had been a hipster long before the term had been coined.

"Mr Bacus?"

"That's me."

"I was given your name by Marjorie Stock at the village store. I'm looking for a new accountant?"

"In that case, you've come to the right place." He opened the door wider. "I've been an accountant for over fifty years now. Would you care to come inside?"

"Thank you."

The house was spotless, but I felt as though I'd stepped through a time warp. Everything about it shouted the fifties.

"Come through to my office, would you?" His office was in the front room and overlooked the overgrown garden. His desk, an antique very similar to my own, was positioned next to the window. "Do have a seat." He pointed to an old, brown leather sofa.

"Thanks."

Mr Bacus sat on a chair next to the desk, which was on castors, and then propelled himself across the room towards me.

"So, young lady, you're looking for an accountant?"

"That's right. My previous accountant went to live in France."

"I spent some years in France when I was younger. It's much too hot for my liking—it made my nose peel something awful. What line of business are you in—err—I'm sorry, I don't even know your name."

"Jill. Jill Maxwell. My family and I recently moved into the old watermill."

"Myrtle Turtle's old place?"

"That's right."

"Lucky you. It's a charming property."

"Thank you. And to answer your question, I'm a private investigator."

"How very interesting."

"The thing is, Mr Bacus, I'm —"

"Do call me Arthur."

"The thing is, Arthur, I'm not particularly good with paperwork, as you'll see from this lot."

"Let me have a look at it." He took the carrier bag, shot back across the room on the chair, and emptied the contents onto the desk. "Receipts, bills, invoices. All the usual suspects. This will be no problem at all. I could whip this into shape for you within a few days, unless you need it sooner than that."

"A few days would be fantastic." I glanced around the room and realised there was no sign of a computer. "Can I ask, Mr Bacus, what do you use to produce the accounts? Is your computer in another room?"

"A computer? Certainly not. I have no use for one of those."

"Do you do it all on a calculator?"

"No, it's all done up here." He tapped his forehead with his finger.

"You do it all in your head?"

"Yes, and I have done ever since I started. I'm proud to say that I've never had any complaints. Is that going to be a problem?"

"Not at all."

"Excellent. Any more questions?"

"No, not really."

"Super. Would you like a drink before you go? I'm afraid I don't have tea or coffee, but I was just about to make myself some Horlicks."

"No, thanks. I'd better get going. When shall I call back?"

"Everything will be ready for you on Friday."

"Great. I'll see you then."

Chapter 17

The next morning, over breakfast, Florence was giddy with excitement.

"Wendy said she's going to make a bracelet for me, Mummy."

"That's very kind of her, isn't it? Are you looking forward to going to her house later today?"

"Yes. Do you think I'll like the dinner that her mummy makes?"

"I'm sure you will." I turned to Jack. "What are the arrangements?"

"I'm going to meet Florence out of school, and walk with her and Wendy's mum back to their house. I'll tell Donna we'll pick Florence up at six-thirty."

"Sounds like a plan. We'll be able to have dinner by ourselves for once."

"I suppose we *could* do that." He flashed that wicked smile of his. "Unless, of course, we think of something better to do instead."

"No wonder you were so enthusiastic about this play date. I should have known." Just then, the letterbox rattled. "It's a bit early for the post, isn't it?"

The postman rarely showed his face before ten in Middle Tweaking.

Jack went through to the hall to collect it. "It isn't the post. It's a flyer for that new hotel. It opens the weekend after next."

"They've cracked on with that."

"It's now called Hotel First Time, and they're holding an open day on Monday, just for the locals. It says they'll be putting on drinks and snacks. We should check it out."

***

I drove straight to Tweaking Manor where I was going to interview Caroline's son, Dominic. As always, it was Mulgrave who greeted me at the door.

"Hello again, madam. Do come in. I believe you're here to see Mr Dominic today."

"That's right. Are we in the Marble Room again?"

"Actually, no. Her Ladyship had to go out, so she said you should use the dining room."

"That's good news. Has the fire been lit, Mulgrave?"

"Indeed it has. I did it myself, first thing this morning, so it should be nice and warm in there by now. I'm afraid Mr Dominic hasn't arrived yet, but if you'd care to go through, I'll make you a cup of tea."

"That would be fantastic, thanks."

The dining room was certainly much more welcoming than the Marble Room, and the cup of tea hit the mark nicely. I wasn't sure what to expect from Caroline's son. So far, the Tweaking family members had been something of a mixed bag. Elizabeth Judge, Caroline's sister, was delightful. Ransom, Caroline's brother, on the other hand, was a horror show.

As it turned out, I didn't have to wait long to find out because I'd only just finished my tea when Dominic arrived.

"I'm so very sorry to have kept you waiting," he said. "There were three sets of roadworks on the way over here."

"That's quite alright." He joined me at the dining table.

"Thank you for coming over today, Dominic."

"Not a problem. When my mother explained that you'd be interviewing all the family, it seemed like the most sensible arrangement. Although, I have to be honest with you, I'm not sure I'm going to be of much help."

"We'll see. Perhaps you could start by telling me if you have any theories as to who might have taken the goblet."

"None at all, I'm afraid. My understanding has always been that it isn't very valuable, and it's certainly an eyesore. Every time I go into the games room and see it, I wonder why my mother insists on keeping it out on display."

"Speaking of the games room, I understand you played billiards with Ransom in there that night."

"Yes. We quite often have a game. We both like to get away from the women's gossip. No offence."

"None taken. Ransom told me that he won."

"Ransom's a liar, then. He's useless at billiards. I beat him every time, even though he does his best to cheat. That particular night, he'd had a skinful, so he was even worse than usual."

"He was drunk?"

"Not falling down drunk, but he'd had one too many. That's how the goblet got knocked over."

"I haven't heard about that."

"Ransom was messing about with his cue, swinging it around like an idiot. He caught the goblet and knocked it onto the floor."

"Was it damaged?"

"No. Except that the base became dislodged. It took Ransom an age to get it back on again."

"But it was okay?"

"Yes. I made sure because I wasn't going to take the

blame for his stupidity. If it had been damaged, I would have told mother it was his doing. But there wasn't so much as a scratch on it."

"And the goblet was definitely still in the room when you'd finished playing billiards?"

"Yes. In fact, we left the games room straight after the incident with the goblet."

"I assume you're aware of the legend?"

"The parchment?" He laughed. "That thing is a joke. No one takes it seriously. I don't know why mother insists on keeping it on the wall. It belongs in the bin."

"Mulgrave showed me one of the secret passageways."

"They're cool, aren't they? I used to love hiding in those when I was a kid. I spent ages trying to find the missing one, but with no luck."

"Your mother doesn't believe it exists."

"She's probably right. Mind you, Mulgrave might know differently."

"Mulgrave? What do you mean?"

"There's long been a rumour that he knows its whereabouts, but if he does, he's never given it up."

"Do you believe that?"

"No. Ransom has never liked Mulgrave. I think he started the rumour in the hope it would get him the sack."

"It clearly didn't work."

"No. Mother thinks too much of him."

***

I arrived at the office to find Mrs V sporting the poncho I'd seen her knitting the previous week.

"What do you think of it, Jill?" She gave me a little twirl.

"It's very colourful, isn't it?"

"I decided to use all the oddments of wool I've had lying around the house. I think it's turned out rather well."

"Who's it for?"

"Me of course. Do you think it suits me?"

"Err — it's — err — lovely."

"Mr Edwards called in about half an hour ago."

Oh, bum! Did that mean he'd not yet given up on the case?

"What did he want?"

"He popped in to settle his account, but I told him that his invoice hadn't been prepared yet. He said not to worry, and that if we put it in the post, he'd pay it by return."

"He really needn't have come into the office just to pay the bill."

"The main reason he came was to bring you some flowers. They're in your office. He said they were by way of a thank you for the work you've done."

Now I felt even worse. Rusty was such a nice old man, and I couldn't help but feel that I'd let him down. But, in all honesty, I didn't know what else I could have done.

The flowers were in a vase on my desk; they were beautiful and must have cost a pretty penny.

"Far be it from me to interrupt your busy day," Winky said. "But there are three cats over here who are dying of hunger."

Agent Ricardo and Officer Lulu were taking a break from their surveillance and were resting on the sofa.

"Sorry, I was just admiring the flowers."

"Never mind the flowers. We're starving. What time do you call this to start work?"

"I had to call in at Tweaking Manor."

"That's all very interesting I'm sure, but it doesn't get us fed, does it?"

"Okay, okay." I went over to the cupboard, took out a can of salmon and emptied it into the bowls. "How much longer is this operation likely to last? Any idea yet?"

"Still hard to say. We'll keep you posted."

I'd only been at my desk for a few minutes when Mrs V came through.

"Why are those cats still here?"

"I — err — they'll be leaving soon."

"I've got the lady from Bubbles here to see you."

"Oh?" I followed Mrs V through to the outer office.

Farah Close was wearing a green smock with a huge paw print on the front.

"Jill, I hope you don't mind me popping in like this. I just wanted to apologise for Monday. I didn't expect so many people to take up the opening offer. I understand they were blocking the stairs for most of the day. I'm really sorry for any inconvenience that might have caused you."

"Don't give it a second thought, Farah. I'm sure it was only a one-off."

"It definitely was. As a token of my appreciation for your understanding, I'd like you to have this voucher. It entitles you to half-price grooming for the rest of the year."

"That's very generous, but it really isn't necessary."

"It will make me feel better. You can use it for either of

your dogs."

"Thanks very much."

"Right, I'd better get back. I mustn't keep Fluffoo waiting."

"*Fluffoo?*"

"She's a beautiful little Pomeranian. It's just a pity about her temper."

***

I'd been giving some thought to what the bank robber, Darren Black, had told me about his accomplice. 'Romeo' apparently considered himself to be something of a ladies' man; he'd admitted to Darren that he regularly used a dating agency here in Washbridge.

It was several years since I'd been in contact with the good people over at Love Spell. The last dealings I'd had with them was when Hilary had called on my help because Armitage, Armitage, Armitage, and Poole, who had moved into the same building, were trying to force her out of her offices. I'd been only too happy to help, and I'd soon put a stop to Gordon Armitage and his evil designs.

I wasn't sure if Love Spell were still at the same address, or if they were even still in business, but I figured a walk in the fresh air would do me the power of good. It turned out not to be a wasted journey because Love Spell's name was on one of the many plaques at the entrance to the building.

The last time I'd visited their offices, the reception desk had been manned by a delightful young man named Nathaniel. Today, though, it was a different young man who greeted me with a warm, welcoming smile.

"Welcome to Love Spell. Do you have an appointment?"

"Actually, no. Does Nathaniel still work here?"

"Nathaniel? No. He left two years ago. My name is Raymond."

"Pleased to meet you, Raymond. I'm Jill Maxwell. I wonder if I might have a word with Hilary, if she's in. We're friends from way back."

"She is in today, but she's with a client at the moment." He checked his watch. "She should be done in another five or ten minutes, and her next appointment isn't for another hour after that. If you'd care to take a seat, I'll check if she can see you as soon as she's free."

"That's great, thanks."

I took a seat and picked up one of the magazines. It turned out to be an arts and crafts magazine. The cover article on decoupage brought back bad memories, so I put it back on the coffee table.

A few minutes later, a young witch came out of the door behind Raymond. As soon as she'd left, he got on the phone and told Hilary that I was in reception. Even before he'd put the phone down, she came charging through the door.

"Jill Maxwell, it's so lovely to see you. How long has it been?"

"A few years."

"Where have you been hiding? A little bird told me that you have a beautiful young daughter."

"I do. Her name's Florence. She's five now and she's just started school."

"Goodness me. How time flies. And why haven't you

brought her in to see me?"

"I will do. I promise. I've just been so busy."

"Are you still running the PI agency?"

"Yes. Jack left the police force and he works from home now."

"You seem to have things well organised. Why don't you come through to my office, and we can catch up? Raymond, would you make us a cup of tea, please? If memory serves me right, Jill has one and two-thirds spoonfuls of sugar."

"You have a remarkable memory, Hilary." I laughed. "But actually I don't take sugar at all now."

At which news, Raymond looked quite relieved.

Over tea, we caught up on each other's news, and then I moved onto the reason for my visit.

"So, Jill, you think this Romeo character is using a dating agency somewhere here in Washbridge?"

"I believe so. I realise Love Spell only handles witches who are looking for partners, but I thought you'd know if there was another agency in Washbridge that accepted wizards onto their books."

"You're a little behind the times. Since you were last here, we've expanded the business. We now find partners for both witches and wizards."

"In that case, there must be a chance that this guy is on your books."

"A very good chance, I'd say. We're the only agency in the Washbridge area that deals with sups since Love Bites closed. I don't suppose you know his real name, do you?"

"I'm afraid not, but I do have this." I took the photo out of my handbag and passed it to her.

"I don't recognise him, but then I mainly deal with witches. My partner, Christie, who you won't have met, deals with the wizards. Unfortunately, she's on holiday this week, but it's just possible that Raymond may remember him. I'll go and check." She disappeared out of the door and came back a few minutes later. "You're in luck. Raymond did recognise the guy and we've managed to pull up his file. It looks like he's triggered our three-strikes policy."

"What's that?"

"We have to be careful not to encourage those who are just looking for one-night stands. We're all about long-term relationships. If a client has three consecutive dates that turn out to be one-night stands, we insist they wait a month before we'll set them up on another date."

"Are you saying this guy is banned from having any more dates?"

"He has been, but his ban ends tomorrow. He's obviously keen because according to Raymond, he's already been in touch to ask about another date."

"Has he really? That's handy."

"Sorry?"

"I have an idea that I'd like to run by you."

Chapter 18

In advance of my visit to CASS, I'd called ahead and spoken to the headmistress. She had been kind enough to book a small study room in the library where I could meet with Maxine Pearldiver.

When I arrived at the library, the study room door was unlocked, but there was no sign of Maxine, so I took a seat and waited. A few minutes later, a young girl came bursting through the door. Maxine Pearldiver was the spitting image of her mother.

"It's such an honour to meet you!" She gushed.

"It's very nice to meet you too, Maxine."

"I'm a massive fan of yours. I have your poster in my locker, and I've watched all the tournaments you've been in."

"I'm flattered. Why don't you take a seat and we can chat?"

"Okay." She put her satchel on the desk. "Before we start, Mrs Maxwell, would you—"

"Please call me Jill."

"Is that okay? Really?"

"Yes, I'm not on the teaching staff at the moment."

"Okay, Jill. Before we start, do you think you could possibly sign something for me?"

"An autograph? Yes, of course."

"Fantastic!" She opened her satchel, pulled out a pile of photographs, and slid them across the desk to me. There must have been at least fifty of them.

"You want me to sign *all* of these?"

"Yes, please. If you don't mind. When the others heard I was going to be speaking to you, a lot of them asked if I'd get them an autograph." She handed me a pen.

"O—kay. Why don't we chat while I'm signing them?"

"Sure. Mum said that you wanted to talk to me about your little girl."

"That's right. Her name's Florence. She's five years old and has just started school in the human world."

"Does she know she's a witch?"

"Yes, she does."

"That's good. Did you know my mum didn't tell me I was a witch until the invitation from CASS arrived?"

"Yes, she told me. In fact, that's one of the things I wanted to talk to you about today. I wondered how you felt about that."

"When I found out, I was really angry. I'm still a little angry, but I realise now that she was doing it with the best of intentions. But she definitely got it wrong. I should have been told from day one. When I eventually found out, it came as a massive shock. And, as if that wasn't bad enough, I suddenly had to decide whether or not to attend CASS."

"That can't have been an easy decision for you."

"It wasn't, but I figured it was too good an opportunity to pass up."

"How was it? When you started at CASS, I mean."

"I found it very difficult at first because I was still trying to come to terms with the idea that I was a witch."

"I imagine the fact that you hadn't been taught any magic didn't help?"

"That was the worst part. When I first got here, most of the other kids had spent their whole life in the paranormal world and had practised magic since they were young. I was starting from scratch. Some of the kids, not all of them—just the cruel ones, used to make fun of me because I was so far behind. There were times when I just wanted to give up and go home."

"But you stuck it out. That says a lot about your character. Have things improved since then?"

"Yes, it's much better. I'm up to speed now. In fact, I'm a better witch than some of those who have been practising magic all their lives."

"Well done, you."

"Are you teaching Florence any spells?"

"So far, I've only taught her three. I'd planned to wait until she was older before teaching her anymore."

"No! You mustn't do that! Sorry for shouting, but that's not fair on Florence. She's a witch, and she should be practising magic. Will Florence join CASS when she's old enough, if she gets an invitation?"

"I'm not sure. I'm going to have to give that some serious thought." I signed the last of the photographs and pushed them across the desk.

"Thanks for doing that, Jill."

"No problem. Thank you for talking to me. It's been very helpful. Very helpful indeed."

***

I was desperate for a coffee and a blueberry muffin.

What? Signing photographs is really hard work, especially when there are thousands of them.

I magicked myself back to the human world and headed straight for Coffee Animal. Although the revamped shop had been open for a few weeks, the sign on the door said that today marked the first day of the 'full' launch.

Whatever they had planned for Coffee Animal, it couldn't be any worse than Coffee Triangle with its awful cacophony of percussion instruments. Coffee Games had been a slight improvement, but that too had been tedious at times, particularly on days such as Simon Says or Blind Man's Buff.

"Welcome to Coffee Animal's launch day." The young woman behind the counter had a pink bow in her hair and a beauty spot on her left cheek. "My name is Dot."

"Hi, Dot. I'm Jill."

"Is this your first visit?"

"Actually, no. In fact, I was here on the day of the siege."

"Oh dear. How terrible for you. I hope you're okay."

"I'm fine, thanks, but I have to admit I'm still a little confused by the choice of name. Coffee Animal? What does that mean, exactly?"

"Have you heard of cat cafes?"

"Yes, I've actually been in a couple."

"Coffee Animal takes that concept one step further. Instead of having cats in the shop all the time, we'll be having a different animal each day." She reached under the counter and brought out a tiny cage. "This is today's animal."

"A hamster?"

"A lot of people make that mistake. It's actually a gerbil."

"Err, right, thanks."

"What can I get for you to drink?"

"A caramel latte please, and do you have any blueberry muffins?"

"You're in luck. We only have one left."

It was a bit of a struggle, carrying the coffee, the muffin, and the cage containing the gerbil, but I managed to find a table next to the window. I didn't think it would be hygienic to put the cage on the table, so I placed it on the seat next to me.

I'd just taken a bite of the muffin when a little voice said, "Hey, can I have some of that?" Sometimes the ability to talk to animals was a curse. "I've been stuck in this cage all day and no one's thought to give me any food."

"I'm not sure that muffins are suitable for gerbils."

"Of course they are. I love them, particularly blueberry ones. Go on, please."

"Okay, then."

"Make sure it has a blueberry in it."

I broke off a piece of muffin and passed it through the bars.

"Is that all I get?"

"Sheesh, some people are never satisfied." I gave him another piece.

"Thanks. My name is Jimbob, by the way. What's yours?"

"I'm Jill." I suddenly became aware of a middle-aged couple who'd stopped by the side of my table and were giving me a very puzzled look.

"Hi," I flashed them my *nothing to see here* smile.

"Did you just tell that gerbil your name?" the man said.

"Yes, it's only polite to introduce yourself, don't you think?"

The woman took the man by the arm and led him away. As she did, I could hear her muttering something about a *crazy woman.*

***

When I got home, Jack was alone in the house because Florence was over at Wendy's house.

"How did you get on at CASS?" Jack said. "Did you get to talk to Maxine?"

"Yes, she seems very nice. After listening to what she had to say, I'm glad that Florence does know she's a witch. Poor old Maxine only found out just before starting at a new school. That made everything twice as difficult for her."

"Is she okay now?"

"Yeah, she seems to be, but she had a really hard time at first. All the other kids had been practising magic for years, and she had to start from scratch. Kids being kids, some of them made her life a misery for a while. I don't want that for Florence."

"What do you suggest we do, then?"

"I think we should allow her to learn more spells now. Then, if she does get an invitation from CASS, she—"

"You know how I feel about that, Jill."

"I know, and we don't have to make a decision about CASS right now, but we do have to allow Florence to be a witch. To learn and practise magic. And she has to start spending time in the paranormal world."

"Okay."

"*Okay*? Just like that?"

"Yes. You're the witch in this family. I have to trust your instincts on this, but I do have one condition."

"What's that?"

"You have to be the one to teach and supervise her. I

don't want your grandmother getting involved."

"No arguments from me there."

"Now that's settled, and we have the house to ourselves, what do you fancy for dinner?"

"Come upstairs and I'll show you."

***

Jack and I were on our way to Donna's house to collect Florence.

"I'm starving," Jack said. "Can we pick up something to eat on the way back?"

"You've just had 'dinner'." I grinned.

"Yes, and very nice it was too. That's one of the reasons I'm so hungry."

There was no answer at Donna's, but there was definitely someone in because we could hear raised voices coming from the other side of the door.

"I hope that isn't Wendy and Florence falling out," Jack said.

"That's not Florence's voice." I knocked again.

This time, Donna opened the door. Standing behind her was a young girl, aged about ten or eleven, who was clearly unhappy about something. "But, Mum, it isn't fair!"

"I'm sorry about this," Donna said. "Do come in."

"Mum, please!"

"Rachel, I'm not going to tell you again. Go up to your bedroom or there'll be no pocket money for the rest of the month."

"It's not fair! Everyone else has got at least three."

"Your room! Now!"

The girl shot upstairs, in floods of tears.

"I'm so sorry you had to witness that. That's Rachel, Wendy's older sister. I sometimes think Wendy can be a handful, but compared to Rachel, she's a little angel. That outburst was all because I refused to buy her another charm for that stupid bracelet of hers."

"My niece has just had one of those."

"All the girls in Rachel's class have got them; it's the latest craze. The bracelets are quite cheap. It's the charms that they sting you on; they're incredibly expensive. That tantrum was all because I'd just told her she can't have another one until next month. She thinks we're made of money. Anyway, enough of my problems."

"Has Florence been okay?" I asked.

"Yes, she and Wendy have played together really nicely. I'll just nip upstairs and get her for you."

Moments later, Florence came charging down the stairs, followed by Wendy and then Donna.

"Look, Mummy," Florence held out her hands. "Wendy made me two bracelets. Aren't they pretty?"

"They're beautiful. You're very clever, Wendy."

"Mummy bought me the bead kit for my birthday." She beamed. "I could make one for you too if you like."

"Maybe another day, Wendy," Donna said. "Florence and her mummy and daddy have to go home now."

"Say thank you to Wendy and her mum for letting you come over," I said to Florence.

"Thank you. I've had a lovely time."

"It was our pleasure."

Jack took Florence by the hand and led her out of the door. I was just about to follow when Donna said, "Jill, I'm so pleased that Wendy has found such a good friend in Florence. I do hope you'll let her come over again soon."

"Of course, and Wendy must come to our place too."

Chapter 19

The next morning, Jack and I were at the kitchen table, eating breakfast. Florence had already finished her cornflakes and was out in the garden. She was throwing the ball for Buddy who was half asleep and less than enthusiastic about the early morning exercise.

"When are you planning to tell Florence what we decided last night?" Jack said. "About her learning more spells?"

"I think that's something we should talk to her about together."

"Are you sure you're okay with that?"

"Yes, she has to know this is something we're both signed up to."

"I hate that there's a large part of her life that I can play no part in."

"I know it's hard for you, but trust me, it's just as hard for me being out at work every day while you're here with Florence."

"I know. When shall we have the conversation?"

"I thought we could do it tonight."

"I don't think that's going to work. We've got the amdram play. Had you forgotten?"

"No, of course not." Although, I'd tried very hard to. "Can't we just cancel?"

"No, we can't. We've promised Kathy and Peter we'll be there."

"Did you remember to contact the babysitter?"

"Yes. Sarah will be here in plenty of time."

"In that case, why don't we talk to Florence now? I don't have to rush out to work this morning."

"Okay, I'll call her in." Jack went over to the door. "Florence! Mummy and Daddy would like to talk to you."

She came running into the house. "Is it time for school?"

"Not yet. Why don't you come and sit at the table with us?" I patted the seat next to mine. "We want to talk to you about magic."

"I've been practising my three spells, Mummy. I'm very good at them now."

"I know you are. You're doing really well. That's why we've decided that you can learn some more."

"When?"

"We'll start next week."

"Will Great Grandma be teaching me?"

"No, she won't!" Jack snapped, causing Florence to flinch. "Sorry, pumpkin, Daddy didn't mean to shout. Mummy will be teaching you."

"What spells will I learn?"

"We'll have to have a think about that," I said. "I'll look through the spell book over the weekend and pick out those that I think will be most suitable."

"I wish I could tell my friends that I can do magic." She sighed. "They would like it."

"You can't do that, darling. We've talked about this before. It's very important that you never tell anyone. Do you promise?"

"I promise."

"There's something else too, Florence. You know Great Grandma, Aunt Lucy and the twins live a long way away, don't you?"

"That's why we can't go to their house, isn't it?"

"Something you don't know is that Aunt Lucy and the twins are witches. Just like you, me and Great Grandma.

They all live in a place called Candlefield."

"I had some candles on my birthday cake, Mummy, didn't I?"

"Yes, darling, you had five of them. Do you remember when I told you about sups?"

"I've forgotten what you said. Is it like soup?"

"No. Sups are what you call people who have magical powers. Like witches and wizards."

"Am I a sup, Mummy?"

"Mummy is a sup. Daddy is a human. And you are both."

"Is that good?"

"Yes, it's very good. You're very lucky. Sups can live here or in Candlefield. That's where Great Grandma, Aunt Lucy and the twins live. I thought that you and I could go over there to visit them this weekend."

"To Candlefield?"

"That's right."

"What about Daddy? Can he come too?"

"I'm afraid he can't. Humans can't go to Candlefield."

"That's not fair." She turned to Jack.

"It's okay, pumpkin. I don't mind," he reassured her. "You and Mummy will have a great time there."

"What about Buddy? Can he come with us? Is he a sup?"

"No, Buddy isn't a sup," I said. "He's a pain in the—"

"Jill!" Wisely, Jack cut me off.

***

I was just about to set off to the office when I got a phone call from Caroline. Normally quite composed, she was struggling to speak and clearly upset about something.

"Caroline, slow down a little, please. What's happened?"

"It's Mulgrave, Jill. I just—I just can't believe it."

"What's happened to him?"

"He's dead. I found him hanging in his room."

"Oh no."

"The silly man took his own life. And for what? A goblet? It doesn't make any sense."

"Have you informed the police?"

"Of course. They're on their way over here now."

"I'll come over too. I'll be there as quickly as I can."

I'd only seen Mulgrave the day before, and he'd seemed perfectly fine, no different to any of the other times I'd seen him. What could possibly have happened to cause him to commit suicide? And why had Caroline mentioned the goblet? What did that have to do with anything?

When I arrived at Tweaking Manor, there was a police car parked on the road outside. As I turned into the gate, a uniformed officer flagged me down.

"Sorry, madam, you can't go in there."

"I'm family," I lied. "Carol—err—Lady Tweaking called and asked me to come over."

He spoke into his radio, then waved me through. There were another two police cars parked outside the house, and the front door was wide open. I'd just stepped inside when a plain clothes officer walked up to me. I didn't recognise him, but since Sushi had moved on, I didn't really know anyone at Washbridge Police Station.

"I believe you told my colleague that you're a relative.

Would you mind telling me your name?"

Before I could respond, Caroline had appeared. "I asked this lady to come over, officer. Please move out of the way and let her through."

He hesitated for a moment, but then moved aside.

"Come on, Jill." Caroline took my arm. "We'll go through to the dining room." The room was uncharacteristically cold because the fire hadn't been lit.

"Are you alright, Caroline?"

"I think so." She took a deep breath. "I just need to sit down for a while."

"Take all the time you need."

She took a few minutes to compose herself and then said, "I'm okay now."

"Why don't you tell me what happened?"

"I woke up this morning at the usual time and came downstairs to the dining room. Normally, Mulgrave has a cup of tea waiting for me, but there was no sign of him, and the fire hadn't been set. He's normally so reliable, so I assumed he must be poorly. I went up to his room and knocked a couple of times, but there was no answer, so I tried the door and it was open. I found him hanging from the beam. It was horrible. I almost collapsed."

"I assume it was suicide?"

"What else could it have been? And all because of that stupid goblet."

"That's the part I don't understand. What does the goblet have to do with any of this?"

"It was on his bed. He must have been the one who took it."

"That doesn't make any sense. Even if it was him, why would he take his own life?"

"I have no idea. Guilt, I suppose."

"But he could have just put it back in the games room and no one would have been any the wiser. What motive could he have had for taking it?"

"I don't know. Money maybe? I'd had to cut his wages, but he wouldn't have got much for that ugly thing. This is all so terrible."

The door opened, and Ransom appeared. "I've made a cup of tea for you, Caroline."

"Thank you, dear. That's just what I needed. What about Jill? Did you make one for her?"

"I didn't realise she was here." He glared at me.

"I'm okay, thanks," I said. "I didn't know you were in the house, Ransom."

"Caroline called me first thing and I came straight over. I wanted to make sure she was okay. I'm going to stay here for a few days until this is all sorted out."

"I've told him that's not necessary," Caroline said.

"It certainly is necessary," he insisted. "You've had a nasty shock. I'm going to stay with you until you're back on your feet again." He turned to me. "Thank you for coming over, but you can leave now. I've got this."

Ignoring him, I addressed Caroline, "Before I go, would it be possible to see the goblet?"

"I don't see why not. I put it back in the games room. I probably shouldn't have moved it, but it's too late now."

"Thanks. I'll pop over there."

"I'll come with you," Ransom said.

"There's no need. I know where it is."

"I insist."

We walked in silence across the main hall to the games room. Everything that everyone had said about the goblet was true. It was truly hideous. I picked it up to get a closer look.

"Be careful with that," Ransom snapped. "It's a family heirloom. Put it down!"

"In a minute." I pulled at the base and it came away. "Whoops!"

"What do you think you're playing at?"

"Relax, it isn't broken." I took a quick look at the underside of the goblet. Engraved inside the stem, normally hidden from view by the base, was a long series of numbers.

"Put it down this minute!" he shouted.

"Just a second." I took out my phone, snapped a few photos of the goblet, then reattached the base.

"I think you should leave now."

"Not before I've had another word with Caroline."

"I don't think—"

I had no intention of waiting for his permission, so I hurried back to the dining room.

"What did you make of it, Jill?" Caroline said.

"It's pretty hideous. Is there anything else I can do for you before I leave?"

"I don't think so. I appreciate all the work you've put in. Let me have your invoice as soon as you can, will you? I'll make sure it's paid straight away."

***

Mrs V had arranged her poncho on the desk, and she appeared to be taking a photo of it with her phone.

That was unusual for two reasons: Firstly, I couldn't for the life of me think why she would want a photo of that ugly thing. And, secondly, I'd not seen Mrs V with a mobile phone for years, let alone taking a photograph with one.

"Good morning, Jill."

"Morning, Mrs V, what are you up to?"

"I'm taking a photo of the poncho, and then I'm going to post it online."

"I didn't think you had a mobile phone. Didn't you give the last one to Armi years ago?"

"That's right, dear. I've never really seen the need for one since then, but after Maud Mizus showed me what she'd done, I thought I might as well give it a go, so I called in at Yarn and Phones."

"*Yarn and phones?*"

"They're very good. They stock a wide selection of yarn, and they also sell mobile phones. The young lady there was most helpful. She had me up and running in no time. It's not nearly as complicated as Maud said it would be."

"Good for you, Mrs V."

"It's amazing. I've posted lots of photos already. Other people can *like* them and add comments. They can even share them with their friends. Take yesterday for example, I posted a picture of the cuckoo socks I'd knitted for Armi. That photo has already had twenty-three likes and one share. And, best of all, I already have thirty followers."

"That's — err — great. I assume you're posting them to your Instagram account?"

"Insta — what, dear?"

"Instagram."

"I can't say I've heard of that one. I'm posting them on YarnAgram. Would you like to see them?" Before I could say no, she held out her phone, and started to flick through them. There were photos of all manner of yarn creations: socks, scarves, jumpers, and of course the now infamous poncho.

"They're all very nice."

"I've decided to spend this weekend uploading photos of all the scarves, jumpers, and socks that I've knitted over the last twelve months. Just think how many followers I'll get then."

"It sounds like you're going to be busy."

"Would you like to know my YarnAgram name, Jill?"

"Sure."

"I'm called TheYarnLady. I thought someone might have already nabbed it, but it was still available."

"That's great. Anyway, I'd better crack on."

Winky was sitting on the windowsill, looking out of the window. He was on his phone and he clearly hadn't heard me come in. I was just about to shout good morning when I heard him say, "Yeah, she really fell for it, but then she always does. CI5, brilliant. And those badges? Where did you get them? A lucky bag? Really? Too funny. That's okay, Lulu, anything for a friend. I'll see you and Ricardo next time you're in town."

I'd heard enough, so I cleared my throat to catch his attention.

Horrified, he turned around, and gabbled into the phone, "I have to go."

"Morning, Winky."

"Morning." He jumped down from the window and up onto my desk.

"Who were you talking to?"

"Nobody. Just an old friend."

"I suppose you'll be ready for some salmon."

"Yes, please."

"No chance."

"What do you mean, *no chance*?"

"I mean, *no chance*. You can't have any. In fact, there's no salmon for you for a month. You're back on the budget food."

"Why?"

"Because I heard what you said. Ricardo and Lulu aren't cops, are they?"

"I—err—"

"And there's no such thing as CI5, is there?"

"Well, I—err—"

"You might as well admit it, I heard everything."

"It was only a joke. Surely you can see the funny side."

"Of course I can, but there's still no salmon for you for a month. I'm sure you'll see the funny side of that too."

Chapter 20

My phone rang and I could see from caller ID that it was Hilary from Love Spell.

"Jill, we're all systems go."

"That was quick."

"Just as I expected, Romeo was in touch the minute his ban expired, very keen to arrange his next date. The only problem is that it's tomorrow at one o'clock. Does that work for you?"

"I'll make it work. This guy needs taking off the streets as soon as possible."

"He chose a witch named Griselda Longribbon from our books."

"Griselda Long—?"

"Ribbon. I'll send you her details and photo over now."

"Where am I supposed to meet him?"

"Do you know Bar Loco?"

"I've never heard of it."

"You know that new office complex they built where the old market hall used to be?"

"Yeah."

"The ground floor has been set aside for bars and restaurants. Bar Loco is the first one to open."

"Okay. I'll find it."

"Be careful, Jill. If this guy is half as bad as you said, he could be dangerous."

"Don't worry. I'll be fine."

"Will you let me know how you get on?"

"Of course I will."

***

It was late afternoon, and I was thinking of calling it a day. We had the amdram play that evening, so we were going to have an early dinner. I was just on the point of leaving when Mrs V came through to my office.

"Jill, there's a Mrs Elizabeth Judge out here. She wondered if you could spare her a few minutes?"

What was Elizabeth doing here?

"Yes, of course. Send her through, would you?"

Elizabeth, who was clearly flustered, hurried into the room. "Thanks for seeing me, Jill. I assume you've heard about Mulgrave?"

"Your sister called me over to the manor this morning. I have to admit I didn't see that coming at all. Mulgrave seemed fine when I saw him yesterday."

"Something about this doesn't ring true."

"What do you mean?"

"Ransom is acting very peculiarly. Did you know he planned to stay on at the manor house?"

"Yes, I saw him this morning, and he said he was going to stay with your sister for a few days to make sure she was okay."

"That's a joke." Elizabeth scoffed. "He's never shown the slightest interest in her wellbeing before. Whenever she's been poorly, I've always been the one to look after her. Why the sudden about-turn? That's what I'd like to know. But it's not just that, Jill. I'm finding it really hard to believe that Mulgrave would have taken his own life."

"What exactly are you suggesting? Do you think someone might have murdered him?"

"I don't know what to think."

"Did you know the goblet was found in his room?" I

said. "Maybe the guilt at what he'd done overwhelmed him?"

"I don't buy that. I simply can't convince myself that Mulgrave would have taken the goblet in the first place."

"Did you mention your suspicions to the police?"

"Yes, for all the good it did. They seem to believe it's a straightforward case of suicide. That's why I came to see you."

"What exactly is it you want me to do?"

"Keep an eye on my sister and try to find out what really happened to Mulgrave."

"Caroline has told me to consider the case closed."

"Don't worry about that. I'm quite happy to pay you from this point on. I just don't want anything to happen to my sister. Will you do it?"

"Of course. I'll go around there tomorrow and see what I can find out."

The truth was, I shared Elizabeth's concern for Caroline, and I certainly didn't trust Ransom.

"Thank you, Jill."

"Before you go, could I ask you something?"

"Yes, of course. Anything."

"Mrs Jones told me she heard you and Ransom arguing on the night of the birthday dinner. Do you remember what that was about?"

"We argue all the time, that's nothing unusual, but yes, I do remember. He accused me of not caring about my sister. He tried to tell me that he was the only one who had her interests at heart. I'm afraid I saw red and let him know exactly what I thought about him."

***

When I pulled up outside the old watermill, there was no sign of Jack or Florence. I'd just got out of the car when I heard someone calling to me.

"Hi there! Hello!" A woman in her early forties waved to me. Sporting a bright orange top, she was struggling to walk due to the combination of high heels and a tight pencil skirt. When she did eventually reach me, she said, "Hi, I'm glad I caught you. My name's Olga. I'm your next-door neighbour."

When we'd lived in Smallwash, our next-door neighbours had lived in the adjoining house. Here in Middle Tweaking, the nearest house was a good fifty yards up the road.

"Pleased to meet you, Olga. I'm Jill."

"We've only recently moved to the village ourselves, about six months ago. We're from the West Midlands." I'd already gathered that from her accent. "I've been meaning to come over and introduce myself ever since you moved in, but I've been so busy that I haven't had the chance. I've seen your husband and your little girl a number of times."

"Jack works from home. You've probably seen him taking and collecting Florence from school. She's just started there."

"We have two children. Olivia is twelve, and Oliver is ten in a month's time. You've probably already seen my husband, Oscar."

"I don't think so."

"He's the postman. We were lucky that he was able to transfer his job down here."

"Do you work, Olga?"

"Not at the moment, but I'm on the lookout. Something

in retail, preferably. If you hear of anything, let me know, would you?"

"Sure."

"I wanted to say we'd love for all of you to come over to our house some time. For a cuppa and cake, maybe."

"That would be nice. Thanks."

"I'd better let you get going. Speak soon, I hope." She turned on her (very high) heels and made her way slowly — very slowly — back up the road.

Jack was all by himself in the lounge.

"How come Florence didn't come to meet me? Is she with Buddy in the garden?"

"No, she's upstairs, in her bedroom. She's been up there for the last thirty minutes."

"What's she up to?"

"I'm not sure. Playing with her toys, I imagine."

"I've just been speaking to our next-door neighbour."

"I didn't realise we had one."

"She lives in the next house up the road. Her name's Olga. She has a weird dress sense but other than that, she seems okay. Her husband is the postman and they've got two kids. A boy and a girl. Twelve and ten, I think. She said we should all go around there for tea and cake sometime."

"Sounds good to me."

"Right then." I put my handbag down. "I'd better go and see what madam is up to."

Florence was lying on her bed, looking through my book of spells. "Mummy, there are so many spells in here."

"You shouldn't be looking at that by yourself. I told you I was going to pick out some spells for you over the weekend."

"I want to learn the 'thunderbolt' spell."

"Definitely not."

"Aww! Why not? It looks fun."

"Because it's very dangerous. You could hurt yourself or someone else."

"But I'd be careful."

"No, Florence. Give me the book, please."

"But Mummy."

"Give me the book now. Magic isn't a game. It's very serious."

"Okay." Reluctantly, she handed it to me.

"I'll pick out some suitable spells over the weekend, and we'll start to learn them on Monday."

***

Jack and I had arranged to pick up Kathy and Peter from their house. Normally, whenever we collected them, they'd keep a look out for us, and by the time we pulled up outside their house, would already be on their way down the drive. Today, though, there was no sign of them.

"Are we early?" Jack checked his watch.

"No, we're dead on time. I'll go and see what they're up to. You wait here."

Even before I reached the door, I could hear raised voices coming from inside: Kathy and Peter were going at it hammer and tongs. When she answered the door, she was red in the face and clearly not a happy bunny.

"Sorry about this, Jill. You'd better come in. I won't be a minute."

"What's wrong?"

"It's Pete. He isn't coming."

"Is he alright?"

"I'm fine." Peter came out of the kitchen. "I'm sorry I can't make it, Jill, but I had a phone call a couple of hours ago from someone wanting a quotation for a big job. I have to have it ready first thing in the morning, so I need to stay in and get it done."

"He should have told them they'd have to wait for their quotation," Kathy said.

"We've been over this," Peter snapped. "Business is really quiet at the moment. I can't afford to turn my nose up at this kind of job."

Just then, Lizzie came out of the lounge with two other young girls about the same age.

"Hi, Auntie Jill."

"I thought you and Mikey would be with your grandparents tonight."

"We were supposed to be, but then Dad changed his mind about going to the play, so he said we could stay here. These are my friends, Rosemary and Lucinda."

Those two had stolen my names!

"I'm very pleased to meet you both."

"Look at our charm bracelets."

All three of them held out their hands.

"They're lovely. You've got a lot of charms on yours, Rosemary."

"Six," she said, proudly.

"I've got four," Lucinda said.

"I've still only got two." Lizzie sighed.

"Yes, Lizzie," Kathy chimed in. "But you've only just had your bracelet. How long have you had yours, Rosemary?"

"Two months."

"See, Lizzie, by the time you've had yours that long, you'll have as many charms as Rosemary."

"No, I won't because she'll have even more by then."

Touché.

I took a closer look at the small charms, which all appeared to be strange little creatures.

"What exactly are these?"

"Elves," Lucinda said.

"All of them?"

"Yes, Jill, that's the whole point." Kathy rolled her eyes at me. "That's why they're called *elf* charms and the shop is called Elf-Charming."

"No two are the same," Rosemary said. "Every charm has an elf in a different pose."

"Considering how much they charge for them, I should think so too." Kathy shook her head. "You'd think for that kind of money they could have given them all different expressions too, but they all look the same. Anyway, come on, Jill, we'd better get going."

"Hold on a minute, Kathy. Girls, do you think I could get a photo of your charm bracelets?"

"What do you want that for?" Kathy shot me a puzzled look. "You're not thinking of buying one for Florence, are you?"

"No, I might get one for myself," I lied. "I'm quite partial to an elf."

The girls were only too keen to allow me to photograph their bracelets. I made sure to get a shot of each of the charms.

I thanked the girls, and then joined Kathy in the back seat of the car.

"Isn't Pete coming?" Jack said.

"No, he has to work." Kathy rolled her eyes.

"I wish I'd come up with that excuse," I said.

"You'll enjoy the play," Kathy insisted.

"I very much doubt that."

In common with every other amateur dramatic production I'd been pressganged into seeing, it was awful. The acting was abysmal, the scenery fell over twice, and the leading lady kept forgetting her lines and had to be prompted from the wings. The leading man, who had at least learned his part, had a dodgy false moustache and beard. There was something about him that looked familiar, but I couldn't put my finger on it.

The interval came as a blessed relief until I discovered there were no refreshments to be had.

"Surely, they could have at least provided ice cream," I moaned.

"The freezer is on the blink, apparently," Kathy said. "What do you think of the play so far? It's good, isn't it? Much better than last year's."

"Thank goodness I didn't see last year's, then."

"Come on, Jill, it isn't all that bad."

"How much longer does it go on for?"

"Another hour, I would think."

I turned to Jack. "If I fall asleep, give me a nudge, would you?"

With only ten long minutes to go, the play was building

to its climax. The leading man and lady had just had a big argument after he'd told her he was leaving her for another woman. When she begged him to stay, he laughed in her face. Then, completely out of the blue, she produced a gun and shot him.

That's when the penny dropped.

After the play had finished, I told Jack and Kathy that they should go home without me.

"Why?" Kathy said. "What are you going to do?"

"There's something I need to do here."

"Like what?"

"It has to do with work. I can't explain now. Jack, I'll see you later."

Before they could ask any more awkward questions, I hurried around the back of the building to the stage door. I didn't have long to wait before the leading man appeared, now minus his false beard and moustache. Moments later, just as I'd expected, the leading lady came out of the door and walked in the same direction. I followed her at a discreet distance until a few minutes later, she climbed into the passenger seat of a red Volvo. The driver, the leading man, leaned over and planted a kiss on her lips.

"Good evening, Mr Smart." I knocked on the driver's side window.

Clearly shocked, he lowered the window. "Who are you? What do you want?"

"Don't you remember me?"

He studied my face for a moment, and then I saw the recognition dawn in his eyes. "You're that fire prevention woman, aren't you?"

"That's me, but I don't work for the fire service. I'm

actually a private investigator."

"Did my wife hire you to follow me?"

"Luckily for you, no. I was hired by a gentleman who lives on the other side of the park from you."

"Why? What does he want from me? And why did you come to my house?"

"My client was looking through his binoculars recently when he saw someone being shot in the master bedroom of your house. If you recall, the police came to ask you about it, and you told them you didn't know anything about it. But that's not true, is it?"

"I have no idea what you're talking about."

"It's time to drop the pretence. The woman he saw in your bedroom was the lady by your side now. Your leading lady."

"Alright, I admit it, but we were just practising our parts. No one was hurt."

"That's as maybe, but I'd bet my last penny that Mrs Smart doesn't know about it."

"Are you going to tell her?"

"That all depends."

"On what?"

"My client has been made to feel very stupid. The police dismissed his claims as the rantings of a senile old man. So, here's the deal. If you don't want me to tell your wife about your lady friend, I'll need both of you to pay a visit to my client. You're going to tell him that he wasn't mistaken in what he thought he saw. You can explain that you were rehearsing for the play."

"What if he tells my wife?"

"He won't. Provided you're totally honest with him, you have nothing to fear. But rest assured, I'll be checking in with him, and if you haven't told him the truth within the next twenty-four hours, I definitely will go to your wife."

I didn't wait for their response, but I was confident that they'd do as I'd asked.

Chapter 21

The next morning, the three of us were at the breakfast table. Buddy, meanwhile, was in the corner of the room, sitting next to his empty bowl, looking daggers at me.

"Mummy." Florence had milk dripping from the corner of her mouth.

"Don't talk with your mouth full."

"But you and Daddy do it."

"Your daddy might, but I'm sure I don't."

"Yes, you do, Mummy. When you were talking to me yesterday, I could see the spaghetti you were eating."

"Yes, well, anyway, what were you going to say?"

"Could I have a bead kit like Wendy's? Then I'll be able to make bracelets for me and my friends."

"If you're a good girl, we'll see."

"I'm a good girl now."

"I know you are, but you have to be a good girl all the time."

"I am a good girl *all* the time."

"I know."

"So, when can I have a bead kit?"

"We'll have a look for one in town the next time we're there."

"When are we going to town again?"

I turned to Jack. "Feel free to help me out here."

"Nah, you're doing just fine." He grinned.

"When, Mummy?"

"Maybe tomorrow."

"Tomorrow, yay! Is it alright if I go out and play with Buddy now?"

"Yes, but I'd better give him some food first or I don't

think he'll be very eager to run after the ball."

I glanced over at the dog who mouthed, "You've got that right."

For a little one, that dog could certainly put away his grub. Within just a couple of minutes, the bowl had been licked clean.

"Come on, Buddy," Florence shouted to him.

"Yes. Go on, Buddy." I nudged him gently with my foot.

"I bet you're glad you went to see that play now, aren't you?" Jack said.

"It was truly awful, but yes because otherwise poor old Rusty would never have learned the truth."

"Do you think they'll go over to his house and admit to him that he did in fact see what he thought he had?"

"I'm absolutely sure they will. It's a choice between that or having his wife find out about his affair. I'm confident Mr Smart would rather face Rusty."

By the time I'd finished my cornflakes, Jack was still only halfway through his bowl of muesli.

"Why do you force yourself to eat that stuff every morning?" I said. "You clearly don't enjoy it."

"Rubbish. I love it." He put a huge spoonful of the mush in his mouth, just to prove his point.

"I'd better be going. I promised Elizabeth Judge that I'd call in at Tweaking Manor to check on her sister."

"What will —"

"Don't talk with your mouth full. That's where Florence gets her bad habits from."

***

When I arrived at Tweaking Manor, there was no sign of the police cars that had been there the day before. The fact that they'd left so soon was a sign that they didn't suspect a crime had taken place.

I rang the doorbell and waited, but there was no response. I knocked with the same result, so I began to thump on the door. After a couple of minutes of non-stop thumping, I heard footsteps coming across the wooden floor. Moments later, the door opened and there stood Ransom.

"What do *you* want?" he snapped.

"I'd like to see Caroline, please."

"You can't. She's in bed, resting, and she's not seeing visitors." He tried to close the door, but I'd already put my foot in the way. "Do you mind?"

"I'm not leaving until I've seen Caroline."

"You look like waiting there all day, then. You're not coming into this house ever again."

"Either you step aside and let me see her or I talk to the police."

"And tell them what, exactly?"

"I'll think of something. Did you know my husband was a police officer?" I didn't think it necessary to mention that Jack had in fact retired. "I'm sure he'll take my concerns seriously."

That clearly gave Ransom pause for thought. "Okay, you can see her, but only for a minute. Then you leave and you don't come back. Understood?"

"Understood."

"Follow me." He led the way across the hall, up the

staircase, and along a corridor. "Caroline is in here. She's asleep, so please don't disturb her."

He opened the door just wide enough for me to see inside. He clearly didn't intend for me to go into the bedroom, but I had other ideas. Before he could stop me, I'd barged past him and made my way over to the four poster bed. Caroline looked several years older than when I'd seen her just the day before.

"Right. You've seen her now." Ransom took my arm. "It's time to leave."

"No chance." I brushed his hand away. "Caroline, it's Jill Maxwell."

Her eyes opened and she blinked a few times before she seemed to register my presence.

"Jill? What are you doing here?"

"I just called in to see how you are."

"I'm okay." She didn't sound it. "Just a little tired. It must be all the upset with Mulgrave."

"Are you sure you're alright?"

"Yes, there's no need for you to worry, I promise."

"Okay, but if you need anything, give me a call."

"I will. Thank you."

"Right," Ransom said. "That's enough. Come on."

He couldn't get me out of that house quickly enough. As I stepped outside, I turned to speak to him, but he slammed the door in my face.

***

When I arrived at the office, Mrs V was staring at her phone and shaking her head.

"What's the matter, Mrs V?"

"How could someone do this, Jill? It's plain wicked."

"What's happened?"

"Someone has whacked my YarnAgram account."

"*Whacked* it? Oh, wait a minute. Do you mean they've *hacked* it?"

"Yes. Look what they've done."

She handed me the phone, which was displaying the photos in her YarnAgram account. At first glance, it looked no different to the last time I'd seen it, but when I scrolled down, I came across a photo of an old pair of socks with holes in the toes. Then a jumper that had one sleeve much longer than the other.

"Where did these new photos come from, Mrs V?"

"I have no idea. I certainly didn't knit those things. Scroll down a little further, there's lots more like that. What will people think if they believe I've made those?"

"Do you have any idea who could have done this?"

"None at all. I'm seriously thinking of quitting YarnAgram altogether. This has got me quite upset."

"I'm not surprised." I handed back her phone.

I felt sorry for Mrs V, but there was nothing much I could do, other than to help her to submit an abuse report to YarnAgram. I wasn't confident that anything would come of it.

Winky was on the sofa, whistling to himself, and looking very pleased with life.

"What have you got to be so happy about?"

"Do I need a reason? I'm just happy to be alive on this beautiful day."

"Just a minute. Was it you? It was, wasn't it?"

"Was *what* me?"

"Did you post those horrible photos to Mrs V's YarnAgram account?"

"What on Earth is *YarnAgram*?"

"Don't play the innocent. You know very well what it is."

"I don't have the foggiest idea what you're talking about."

"Someone has whacked, I mean hacked her account and posted photos of old socks on there."

"And you think I did it?"

"Let's just say you're at the top of my suspect list."

"That's charming. Hang a cat without any evidence, why don't you?"

"I intend to get to the bottom of this and if I find out you did it, there will be consequences."

"And how exactly do you intend to do that? You aren't exactly a computer wizard, are you?"

"No, but I—err—"

"I could find out who did it."

"You? How?"

"I have my contacts."

"Are you being serious?"

"Perfectly. Just say the word and I'll give Nobby the Nerd a call. He'll get to the bottom of it in no time."

"You'd do that?"

"Yes. For a price."

"I might have known. What do you want?"

"You have to raise the salmon ban with immediate effect."

"Okay, but only when your friend has tracked down the culprit."

"Deal. I'll get straight on it." He jumped onto the

windowsill and disappeared out of the window.

***

When Hilary from Love Spell had told me that my date with Romeo was to be at Bar Loco, I'd envisaged a modern hipster joint where all kinds of crazy people socialised.

I'd been completely wrong.

The 'loco' in Bar Loco turned out to be short for locomotive, as in locomotive trains. The whole bar was train themed. Great. Not.

Before visiting the bar, I'd used the 'doppelganger' spell to make myself look like Griselda who was a few years younger than me. And almost as pretty.

What? Of course I'm being completely objective.

I was horrified to see Mr Hosey standing behind the bar. He was dressed in a train driver's uniform, as were all the other staff. I hadn't seen him since we'd left Smallwash, and I certainly hadn't missed him. Thankfully, he had no way of knowing it was me.

"What can I get for you, madam?"

"I'll have a fruit juice, please."

"Are you sure you wouldn't like one of our cocktails? I can recommend the sidings."

"No thanks, just an orange juice."

I'd no sooner got my drink than I saw my quarry walk through the door. Romeo, who was taller than I'd imagined, was clearly dressed to kill. As soon as he spotted me, he flashed me a killer smile, waltzed over to where I was standing, and leaned against the bar in what was clearly a carefully rehearsed pose.

"Hello, beautiful. You're even lovelier than your photograph. And what a lovely name. Griselda. Is that what people call you, or do you go by Griz?"

"Griselda will be fine."

"I bought this for you." He produced a single red rose from behind his back.

"Thank you. You're a bit of a Romeo, aren't you?"

"It's funny you should say that." He grinned. "Romeo is my nickname. What's that you're drinking?"

"Just an orange juice."

"That won't do at all. Why don't I get us some cocktails?"

"Okay. If you insist."

Once we had our drinks, we headed for a quiet booth deep inside the bar. Romeo, whose real name he assured me was Brodie Best, certainly had the gift of the gab. Unsurprisingly, his favourite subject was himself. I smiled sweetly and nodded occasionally as he droned on about his boring life. Curiously, he failed to mention the most significant part. That he was a crook who thought nothing of doing the dirty on his partners-in-crime.

After our third round of cocktails, ninety percent of which I'd managed to pour into the nearby plant pot, he was obviously under the impression that we'd made some kind of connection.

"So, Griselda, what do you say we move on to somewhere else?"

"Sounds good to me. Where did you have in mind?"

"We could go back to my place." He gave me a knowing wink.

"I have a better idea. My apartment is only five minutes away. We could go there."

"Absolutely." His face lit up, and he clearly thought this was his lucky day. "Let's go." He took my hand and led the way out of the bar.

As we walked, he continued to talk nonstop. He told me how much he spent on clothes, how fantastic his apartment was, and about the car he was thinking of buying.

"This is a shortcut," I said. "If we go down here, we'll be at my place in a couple of minutes." I pointed to the alleyway between two office buildings.

"Sure. Let's go."

When we were halfway down the alleyway, I checked that there was no one else around. The coast was clear, so I stuck my foot in front of his and gave him a gentle nudge, which sent him flying onto the floor. He hit the ground with a thump, tearing one knee of his trousers.

"What did you do that for?" He looked at me with a startled expression. "These trousers cost a small fortune."

"Those are the least of your problems, pal." I reversed the 'doppelganger' spell.

"Who are you?"

"I'm the person who's going to put you behind bars."

"You think you can capture Romeo?" He scoffed. "You'll be sorry you messed with me."

He tried to stand up, but I was too quick for him. I used magic to tie his arms and legs, sending him crashing back to the ground.

"Your magic isn't strong enough to hold me." He spent the next few minutes trying to reverse my spell, but he'd underestimated my powers, which were far stronger than his. "You can't do this. Let me go!"

"I don't think so." With the help of the 'power' spell, I

was easily able to pick him up.

"Put me down!"

"Your wish is my command." I walked over to one of the large industrial waste bins, lifted the lid, and dropped him inside. "That's where you belong. With the rest of the rubbish."

"Let me out!" he screamed, as I slammed the lid shut.

I called Daze, who was so excited to hear my news that she dropped what she was doing and came straight over, with Blaze in tow.

"Where is he?" She glanced around. "He didn't get away, did he?"

"No, he's where he belongs." I tapped the waste bin.

"Let me out!" Romeo shouted.

"Well done, Jill." Daze lifted the lid. "That's our guy. We'll take him off your hands."

"Before you do, there's something else I'd like to discuss with you."

"Sure." She turned to Blaze. "Can you take this scumbag back to Candlefield while I talk to Jill?"

"It'll be my pleasure." Blaze climbed onto the bin, took out his net and threw it over Romeo, and the two of them disappeared in a puff of smoke.

"Take a look at these, Daze, and tell me what you think." I held out my phone and showed her the photos I'd taken of the girls' charm bracelets.

"Where did you get these?"

"The bracelets belong to my niece and her friends. Are those charms what I think they are?"

"I have a horrible feeling they might be."

"I was afraid you'd say that. What are we going to do

about it?"

Chapter 22

Mr Bacus, my new accountant, had said I could call around on Friday afternoon to pick up my books. I really wasn't sure what to expect from a man who didn't use a computer or even a calculator to prepare the accounts. He did, however, come highly recommended by the Stock sisters at the local store.

So, it was with some trepidation that I knocked on his door.

"Jill, do come in. I hope you don't mind, but I've got my flies out."

That comment stopped me dead in my tracks. Surely, I must have misheard him.

"Sorry, Mr Bacus, what did you say?"

"I make flies."

"Oh?"

"For fly fishing."

"Of course." I followed him through to the front room which doubled as his office. "I take it you're a fisherman, then?"

"Not at all. It's far too boring. I just enjoy making the flies."

"I see. Do you sell them?"

"No, I make them purely for the fun of it. I have them displayed on the walls of my bedroom. Would you care to see them?"

"Err, actually I'm a bit pushed for time at the moment. Perhaps another day."

"I've been making them for so long I've almost run out of wall space. I've already filled three walls, and I'm halfway across the last one. I'm not sure what I'll do with them once that one is full. Anyway, Jill, you're not here to listen to me talk about my flies. You'll want to see your accounts."

"Yes, please. If they're ready. If not, I can always pop back another day."

"I promised they'd be ready today, and I'm a man of my word." He opened the bottom drawer of his desk and brought out a blue ledger. "Voila!"

I flicked through the pages; a lot of it meant nothing to me, but I could understand the most pertinent information: Profit and loss—a loss, obviously. The money owed to me—not much. Money that I owed—too much. All in all, it painted a pretty depressing picture, but that was nothing unusual.

"That's great, Mr Bacus, did you have any problems with the paperwork I left with you?"

"None at all. It's all filed away neat and tidy in my basement. If you'd rather take it away with you, I can get it for you."

"No, I'm glad to see the back of it. How much do I owe you?"

"That'll be fifty pounds plus VAT, please."

"Right. Is that your monthly charge?"

"No, I don't believe in those. I'll just charge you every time you bring the paperwork in. With your level of turnover, you'll only need to do that once a quarter."

"Right, thanks." That was less than Luther had charged me, and I was certain it was much less than Starr would have expected. "Do you take credit or debit cards?"

"I'm afraid not."

"A cheque, then?"

"I'm afraid it's cash only. Sorry, I should have

mentioned that before."

"Not to worry. I don't actually have that much cash on me at the moment. I've never really taken any notice, is there a cash machine here in the village?"

"There's just the one. It's inside Tweaking Stores."

"I can't say I've noticed it when I've been in there."

"When you walk through the door, turn left and it's at the very bottom near the back wall."

"Right. I'll pop over there now, draw out some money, and be back in a jiffy."

"As you wish, but there's really no hurry. You could drop the money in later if you like."

"I'd rather do it now. I'll only be a few minutes."

I made my way across the village to Tweaking Stores. Once inside, I followed Mr Bacus' instructions, turned left and walked to the far wall, but there was no sign of the cash machine. I was just about to go to the counter to enquire of its whereabouts when I spotted it, hidden behind a pile of plastic buckets. I managed to move them to one side, just far enough to give me access. After I'd put my card in the slot, entered my PIN and the amount I wanted to withdraw, the machine churned away for a few seconds, then beeped and displayed a message that informed me it was out of cash.

I couldn't believe it. This store was beyond useless. Not only did they not have custard creams, bread or butter, but they didn't even have money in their cash machine.

After retrieving my card, I made my way over to the counter where Marjorie Stock was busy writing in the ledger.

"Jill, did you find what you were looking for?"

"Actually, I'm not here to buy anything today. I came in

to withdraw some money, but the cash machine says it's out of cash."

"Oh dear. Someone mentioned it was empty yesterday, but I thought Cynthia had been in touch with the people to get it refilled."

"It's still empty."

"I'm so sorry. How very annoying for you. I'll give them a call straight away. I'm sure it'll be refilled by tomorrow morning. Tomorrow afternoon, at the latest."

"Right. Thanks."

I nipped back to Mr Bacus and explained that I wouldn't be able to pay him until the next day. He was very understanding and said I could drop by anytime with the cash.

There was just one final thing I needed to do.

She answered the call on the first ring. "Starr speaking."

"Hi, it's Jill Maxwell."

"Jill — ?"

"The private investigator."

"Oh yes, of course. Good afternoon. Are you ready for me to go through your accounts and plan your strategy going forward?"

"Actually, no. I'm afraid that I've decided I won't be needing your services."

"Really? That is disappointing. May I ask why?"

"It turns out that there's an accountant a few doors down from me in the village where I live. I've decided to use him because it's much more convenient."

"I see. I trust he's going to review your business strategy, and put a management reporting system in place?"

"Of course. He's got all of that in hand."

"In that case, I wish you the best of luck. You know where I am if you need me."

***

Florence came running up to me as soon as I walked through the door; she was clearly bubbling over with excitement about something.

"Mummy, Daddy says we can go freaky on Sunday."

"Huh? Did he? Let's go and find him, and he can tell me all about it." She took my hand and led me out into the back garden where Jack was trying desperately to get Buddy to run after the ball.

"He won't fetch it for me," Jack said. "He'll do it for Florence, but not for me."

The bargain I'd struck with Buddy was for him to play ball with Florence. If we wanted him to fetch the ball for us too, we'd no doubt have to renegotiate the terms of the deal.

"Florence has just told me that we're *going freaky* on Sunday?"

"Oh yes." He grinned. "She's talking about Freaking Tweaking."

Oh bum! I'd been hoping that we might escape the village on Sunday to avoid that.

"What is Freaking Tweaking?" I asked, all innocent-like.

"It's the annual festival that takes place on Tweaking Meadows," Jack said. "It sounds great."

"Daddy says there'll be lots of rides and games and toffee apples and candyfloss," Florence said.

"Great! How did you happen to hear about it, anyway?"

"Kathy rang about an hour ago to see if we were going. She was surprised I didn't already know about it. You would have thought there would have been posters or flyers, wouldn't you?"

"You would, yeah."

"I told her it sounded great and that we'd definitely be up for it, so she and Lizzie are coming over on Sunday."

"What about Peter and Mikey?"

"Pete has persuaded Mikey to go go-karting."

"Freaky sounds fun, doesn't it, Mummy?" Florence said.

"It sounds absolutely brilliant."

It was my turn to read Florence her bedtime story. I'd tried desperately to persuade her to let me read a different book, but she insisted on the same one again. Her favourite. A story about a worm who wanted to live in a tree. It's hard to adequately describe just how much I hated that stupid book. If you were a worm, why ever would you want to live in a tree where all the birds live? The whole premise was beyond ridiculous.

What do you mean, I'm overthinking it?

Fortunately, Florence fell asleep halfway through the second reading, so I sneaked downstairs.

"Freaking Tweaking sounds brilliant, doesn't it, Jill?" Jack was way too excited.

"Fantastic."

"It's lucky Kathy told us about it. We might have gone out and missed all the fun."

"That is lucky." I was going to kill that sister of mine the next time I saw her. "Jack, now that Florence is asleep, I have to go out."

"Why?"

"I want to check on Caroline. I popped in there this morning and she didn't look very well at all. Her brother's staying with her and I wouldn't trust him as far as I could throw him. I'm worried something really bad might happen."

"Will you be gone long?"

"I don't know. Possibly."

"Be careful, Jill."

"I always am." I gave him a kiss. "Don't wait up for me."

***

I drove to Tweaking Manor, but instead of pulling into the driveway, I parked some distance up the road and made my way back to the house on foot. There was no point in knocking on the door because even if Ransom did answer it, there was no way he'd allow me inside again. Instead, I made myself invisible, and then magicked myself inside the manor house.

Standing in the large hallway, I listened for any sounds of life, but the house was silent. I made my way upstairs to Caroline's bedroom and slipped quietly inside. She looked just as bad as she had earlier, so I walked over to her bedside, to make sure she was still breathing. She was, but she didn't stir. Where was Ransom? He was supposed to be looking after her.

Once I was out of the bedroom, I cast the 'listen' spell. I figured that if there was anyone in the house, it would help me to hear them. The spell did the trick because I could hear a voice in the distance. It sounded like

Ransom, and it appeared to be coming from downstairs somewhere.

Still invisible, I made my way down the stairs and followed the voice to a corridor with doors on either side. I expected the sound to come from one of the rooms, but it didn't. Instead, it appeared to be coming from the very end of the corridor, but that didn't make sense because it was a dead-end. As I stood there, trying to work out what was going on, I heard footsteps on the other side of the wall. Moments later, the wall slid open, and Ransom stepped out. As he walked away, the wall began to slide slowly closed, so I quickly slipped inside.

This was clearly the 'lost' secret passageway; its bare stone walls were illuminated by a series of lanterns. My sense of direction is not the best, but it was obvious even to me that the passageway led outside, under the rear garden. I'd walked at least a hundred yards, and still seen nothing of interest. Where did it lead to, and who had Ransom been shouting at?

I was beginning to think this was a wild goose chase when I saw it: Embedded in the rock wall was a huge vault. So, the legend of the parchment was true after all. There *was* a vault, but it wasn't *in* Tweaking Manor. It was beneath the grounds behind the manor house.

Next to the vault was a small wooden table and a single wooden chair. The table was covered in sheets of paper. As I got closer, I noticed that someone had stuck another sheet of paper onto the wall in front of the desk. On it was a series of numbers, which I recognised as those that had been engraved inside the goblet. The papers on the desk were filled with rows of numbers, each one clearly a different combination of those same numbers. Ransom must have been trying to find the combination that would open the vault. The shouting I'd heard had not been directed at someone else. It must have been out of sheer frustration as his efforts to find the correct combination kept failing. I'm certainly no mathematician, but even I knew there had to be millions of possible combinations. He could be at this for years and still not find the right one.

I heard a sound behind me; it was the wall sliding open again. Ransom was on his way back. What to do? I could have stayed and confronted him, but I didn't feel that I had enough information to act yet. I was still invisible, so I could easily have slipped past him, but I wanted to know where the passageway led to.

I hadn't gone much further before I came to what appeared to be yet another dead end. I was convinced it must be another exit, but how to open the wall? I touched one stone after another, but with no success. Maybe the lanterns? I tried pulling on one of them, but it wouldn't budge. I was running out of options. I tried the next lantern, and eureka, the wall slid open.

I emerged into a thick clump of bushes. As the wall slid closed behind me, I forced my way through the foliage, getting scratched several times for my trouble. Once I was clear of the bushes, I could see the rear of the manor house in the distance. In front of me was a large expanse of grass, which had probably once been a magnificent lawn, but had long since gone to weed.

Under cover of darkness, I made my way back to the car. When I arrived home, Jack was still up.

"How did it go?" he asked.

"Let's just say it proved to be quite interesting."

"How's 'her ladyship'?"

"Not great. I'll need to go back there in the morning, and I'm going to need your help."

Chapter 23

By the next morning, I'd formulated a fantabulous plan.

Once Florence had finished her breakfast and gone outside to play with Buddy, I explained to Jack what I needed him to do.

"I'm not sure about this, Jill."

"Why? What's wrong? It's a fantabulous plan."

"It's dangerous."

"I scoff at danger."

"If anything goes wrong, I'm going to be left with some serious egg on my face."

"You've already got marmalade all over it now, so what's the difference?"

"This isn't a joking matter. I may not be in the police force anymore, but I still have my reputation to think of. If this goes pear-shaped, I could end up being charged with wasting police time."

"Come on, Jack. I know what I'm doing. I need you to trust me on this one."

"Okay, but there's still one big flaw in your plan."

"What's that?"

"Have you forgotten that it's Saturday, and Florence has her dance class this morning?"

Oh bum! "Yes, I had forgotten."

"We can't let her down."

"Of course not, but it's okay, I've got an idea. Wait there." I hurried through to the lounge and made a call. "Is that Donna?"

"Speaking. Jill?"

"Yes. Good morning. I'm sorry to call you so early."

"That's okay. There's nothing wrong, is there? Is

Florence alright?"

"She's fine. I need to ask a really big favour of you."

"Ask away. If I can help, I will."

"Something urgent has cropped up that needs both Jack's and my attention. I don't want Florence to miss her dance class this morning, so I wondered if there was any chance you might be able to take her with you and Wendy?"

"Of course. No problem. I can pick her up on our way past if that's okay?"

"That'll be fine. I'll be out, but Jack will be here. We were planning to drive into Washbridge afterwards, to buy Florence a bead kit like Wendy's. Do you think Wendy would like to come with us?"

"I'll have to ask her, but I'm pretty sure she will."

"That's great. We'll get some lunch while we're there."

"Sounds good. Tell Jack I'll be over in a few minutes."

I went back into the kitchen and told Jack what I'd arranged. Then I popped out into the garden.

"Florence, Mummy has to go to work for a little while."

"Aren't you coming to dance class with me?"

"I can't today. Daddy has to work too."

"Aww! But I'll miss dancing."

"You won't because Wendy's Mummy is going to collect you. You and Wendy can go to dance class together."

"Okay."

"Afterwards, Mummy and Daddy will take you and Wendy to town, to get lunch and to buy your bead kit."

"Wendy's coming with us?"

"Yes, I think so."

"I want chicken nuggets!"

"We'll have to see what Wendy wants. She might not like them."

"Everyone likes chicken nuggets, Mummy."

"I have to go now." I gave her a kiss. "Have a lovely time at dancing."

***

I took a slow drive over to Tweaking Manor, and this time I parked straight in front of the house. I had serious doubts that Ransom would answer the door to me, so I tried a different tack. With the engine still running, I put my hand on the horn and held it there. The sound was deafening. A couple of minutes later, the front door opened, and a red-faced Ransom came charging out of the house, across the gravel, and thumped on the side window.

"Good morning, Ransom."

"What do you think you're playing at? What's all this noise about?"

"I just wanted to get your attention."

"I would imagine you've got the attention of everyone within a five-mile radius. My sister needs rest. How is she supposed to sleep with that racket? What do you want, anyway? I told you never to come back here again."

"I thought it was time that you and I had a little chat."

"About what?"

I climbed out of the car. "Let me think. Oh yes, I know. How about legends?"

"I have no idea what you're talking about. Get back in your car and leave."

"Don't you find the legend of the parchment

fascinating?"

He seemed taken aback for a moment, but he quickly regained his composure.

"That's just stuff and nonsense. Everyone knows that."

"Really? What about the vault that's mentioned in the legend? Do you think that's real?"

"Of course not. There is no vault. It's just a myth."

"We'll see about that, shall we?" Before he could react, I sidestepped him and ran towards the house.

"Hold on! You can't go in there!" He came after me, but I already had several yards start on him.

By the time he'd caught up with me, I was standing at the end of the corridor where I'd been the previous night.

"So, Ransom, is there anything you'd like to tell me?"

"I have nothing to say to you. I want you to leave this house right now."

"I assume you've heard the rumours that Mulgrave knew the whereabouts of the vault?"

"I never listen to rumours."

"Okay. Let's talk about the goblet, then."

"What about it? Mulgrave took it. They found it in his room."

"I'm talking about the night you were playing billiards with Dominic. The night you knocked it onto the floor and the base came off."

"This is getting tiresome. I won't tell you again, it's time for you to leave."

"When the base dislodged, you thought you'd found the combination to the vault, didn't you? Was that the deal you made with Mulgrave? He would show you where the vault was and in return, you'd share the combination?"

"I still have no idea what you're talking about. There is no combination and there is no vault. I've asked you nicely. Now I'm telling you. Leave now or I will personally throw you out of that door."

"No vault, you say?" I pulled on the lantern, and the wall slid open behind me. "Whoops-a-daisy!"

His expression now was one of pure hatred. "You should have left when you had the chance."

"Why? What are you going to do to me, Ransom? Murder me, like you did Mulgrave? That's what happened, isn't it? Once he'd shown you where the vault was, you no longer needed him, did you? Why share the treasure with him?"

"Come here!" He started towards me.

"Stay right where you are." I held up my hand. "If you come any closer, you'll be sorry."

"Don't make me laugh." He scoffed. "I dealt with Mulgrave, and I can certainly deal with a little girl like you."

He was quicker than I'd given him credit for, and before I could block him, he'd pushed me backwards into the passageway. I almost lost my balance but managed to recover my footing. He followed me inside and the wall closed behind him.

"Before you do anything you might regret, Ransom, there's something you should know." I took out my phone, with the intention of telling him that the police had been listening in to our conversation.

Before I got the chance, he laughed. "That won't do you any good. You can't call anyone for help. There's no signal down here."

I glanced at the phone; there were no bars whatsoever,

and the call I'd been on had disconnected. I turned on my heels and ran down the passageway. Only when I reached the vault did I stop, turn around, and face him.

"You do realise you're on a fool's errand, don't you, Ransom?" I pointed to the pile of papers on the desk. "How many combinations have you tried so far? A thousand? Ten thousand? You'll be an old man and you still won't have found the correct one."

"Shut up."

He threw a punch, which I ducked easily. Before he could throw another, I'd cast the 'power' spell, grabbed his arm, and pushed it up his back. When he began to struggle, I pushed him face first into the stone wall, and he crumpled into a heap at my feet.

Although Ransom was a large man, the 'power' spell meant it was easy for me to carry him back to the hallway, where I laid him on the floor and waited. A few minutes later, I heard the sound of sirens and two police cars skidded to a halt on the gravel outside the house. Three uniformed officers got out of one car, a plain clothes officer and Jack got out of the other. Jack came running over and took me in his arms.

"Are you okay?"

"I'm fine. Did you hear Ransom's confession?"

"Yeah, we did, but when the line suddenly went dead, I thought something had happened to you."

"There's no reception down in the secret passageway."

"Where is he?" the detective asked.

"In the hallway, spark out. He's probably going to need an ambulance."

***

We'd not been back at the house for very long when Donna arrived with Florence and Wendy.

"Thank you very much for doing this, Donna," I said. "I owe you one."

"No problem."

"Was Florence okay?"

"She was. They both had a lovely time. Are you sure it's okay for Wendy to go to town with you?"

"Absolutely. We're going to get lunch and then buy the bead kit for Florence. And, if it's okay with you, I'd like to buy Wendy a little something too."

"You don't need to do that, Jill."

"I'd like to, by way of a thank you for this morning. And besides, we can't very well buy something for Florence and not get something for Wendy."

"Okay, but don't spend too much."

On our way into Washbridge, Florence and Wendy were chatting nonstop in the backseat of the car, clearly excited about their little adventure. By the time we'd parked in the city centre, it was almost lunchtime, and Jack and I were starving.

"What does everybody fancy for lunch?" Jack said.

"Chicken nuggets!" Florence shouted.

"What about you, Wendy?"

"I'd like chicken nuggets too, please."

Jack went to the counter while I waited at the table with the two girls. I couldn't believe the size of the bucket he came back with.

"How many have you got there?"

"It's a family size bucket. It has twenty in it."

"We'll never eat all those."

Wendy and Florence didn't need any encouragement to dive in, and they were soon munching on the nuggets. I managed a couple, but I wasn't impressed with them. There was one unexpected highlight when Wendy inadvertently put her elbow on the ketchup and squirted Jack all over his shirt. I really shouldn't have laughed, but it was so funny. And, it made a refreshing change for it to happen to someone other than me.

"It's not funny, Jill."

"I'm not laughing," I said while wiping tears from my eyes.

"Can we go and get my bead kit now, Mummy?" Florence had almost as much ketchup on her face as Jack had on his shirt.

"Yes, darling. Wendy's Mummy told me that she bought hers from Toy Arcade, so we might as well start there. Wendy, you can look for something, too."

"Thank you, Mrs Maxwell."

Even now, all these years later, I still got the heebie jeebies whenever I walked into a toy shop. It took me back to the time I'd had to try and track down a TDO for Lizzie for Christmas. TDO, short for Total Dream Office, had been that year's must-have present. I'd promised Kathy I would get one for Lizzie, but like an idiot, I'd left it too late. In the end, it had been Winky who'd come to my rescue. That cat did have his uses sometimes.

Fortunately, there was no such problem today because the shops had a shelf full of the bead kits. Wendy chose a kit for making sparkly pictures with glitter. I ignored Jack's concerns that her mother might not be too thrilled at having pots of glitter in the house.

On our way back to the car, I spotted the Elf-Charming shop across the road. Daze and I had arranged to discuss the issue of the missing elves again on Monday, but it seemed silly to be so close and not at least take a look at their operation.

"Why don't we go and have a look in there?" I pointed across the road.

"Don't tell me you want one of those charm bracelets?" Jack shot me a puzzled look.

"Why not?"

"After all the things you've said about them?"

"I might let you buy me one for my birthday."

"Lizzie has one of those, doesn't she, Mummy?" Florence said.

"Yes, darling, she does."

"Can I have one?"

"You've already had a toy today, haven't you?"

"Can I have one for Christmas?"

"We'll see."

No expense had been spared on either the exterior or interior of the shop. Inside, everything was white, chrome or glass. Behind the counter, a young woman, wearing a grey suit, greeted me with a smile that looked like it had been painted on.

"Good morning, madam. Do you already have an Elf-Charm bracelet?"

"No, I don't."

"You'll find they're very reasonably priced." She pointed to the display cabinet in front of her.

"So I see." I glanced at the charms. "Those look rather

expensive, though."

"Not when you consider that each one is unique."

Over by the other cabinets, Florence had opened her bead kit, and the two girls were studying the contents.

As I walked past Jack, I said in a hushed voice, "Get ready."

Before he had the chance to ask what I meant, I gave Florence's arm a gentle nudge, causing her to drop the box onto the floor. The beads scattered everywhere.

"Mummy!" she yelled at me. "Look what you've done!"

"Sorry, darling. It was an accident. Daddy will help you pick them up."

Jack joined the girls on their hands and knees, and even the assistant, who'd witnessed the incident, came out from behind the counter to help. That gave me the opportunity I'd been hoping for, so I sneaked through the door at the back of the shop. The contrast there couldn't have been more pronounced: it was dark, dirty and most unwelcoming. I walked down a grimy corridor and came to a large room, which was empty except for several piles of boxes in the far corner.

I was about to turn around and check the opposite end of the corridor when I heard a tiny voice.

"Hello!"

Then another voice. "Please help us."

"Get us out of here!"

Soon, there was a chorus of the tiny voices, which all seemed to be coming from behind the piles of boxes. I hurried over there and found the entrance to another passageway. Next to it, was a metal door behind which were dozens of elves all squeezed into a tiny room.

"You have to get us out of here. They're going to shrink

us. They've already done it to lots of our friends."

"Who are *they*?"

"Two wizards. They're horrible men. They've gone out to get something to eat, but they'll be back any minute."

"Don't worry, I'll get you out. Stand back from the door."

I cast the 'power' spell and pushed the metal door. As soon as it sprang open, the elves piled out.

"Thank you so much, but we need to get to Candlefield before those wizards come back."

"I'll take you there, but first I need you to tell me how they do the shrinking."

"There's a machine down that corridor. I'll show you." He and the other elves led the way to a smaller room. In one corner was a machine the size of an upright freezer. On the front of it was a plaque that read Shrinkometer.

"Once they've shrunk us, they dip us in silver gunk. Please will you take us back to Candlefield now?"

"Okay. Hold each other's hands. You, grab mine." They didn't need telling twice. "Everyone ready?"

"Yes," they chorused.

"Okay, here goes." I didn't have time to think where best to take them, so I plumped for Cuppy C.

Pearl gave me the strangest look. "Jill, where did all these elves come from?"

"Sorry, there's no time to explain. Give them all a cup of sweet tea, would you? I think they need it."

"But, Jill, what — ?"

"Sorry, I have to go."

I magicked myself back to the room with the Shrinkometer, and I was just about to make my way back to the front of the shop when I heard footsteps and voices.

"They've gone!" a male voice said. "All of them. Someone has forced the door."

"That would be me," I shouted.

Moments later, two rough-looking wizards came charging into the room.

"Who are you?" they demanded.

"My name is Jill. I'm very pleased to make your acquaintance."

"What have you done with our elves?"

"I thought I'd save you some time by putting them in there." I pointed to the machine.

They both walked over to the Shrinkometer and pulled open the doors. I sneaked up behind them and pushed them inside.

Then I pressed the big green START button.

Chapter 24

The next morning, Jack and I were fast asleep when suddenly the bedroom door crashed open and in skipped Florence in her Pretty Possum pyjamas. Before I knew what was happening, she'd jumped onto the bed and was bouncing up and down.

"Florence," I said, still half asleep. "What do you think you're doing?"

"It's freaky day, Mummy. Time to get up."

Jack checked the time on his phone. "It's only half past six, Florence."

"Come on, Daddy. Come on, Mummy. Please!"

"Why don't you go back to bed for just a little longer, and let Mummy and Daddy sleep?" I said.

"I'm hungry. Can I have my breakfast, please? Buddy wants his, too."

"I don't think she's going to give up on this." Jack sighed.

"You're right. Why don't you take her downstairs and give her some breakfast while I see to things up here?"

"*See to things?*" He grinned. "You must think I'm stupid. As soon as we're out of the door, you'll roll over and go back to sleep. If I have to get up, so do you."

"If you loved me, you'd let me have a lie in."

"Emotional blackmail isn't going to get you anywhere. Up you get!"

That husband of mine was so selfish sometimes.

As soon as I walked into the kitchen, Buddy started pawing at my bare feet. He would just have to wait.

"I quite fancy a fry-up this morning," Jack said. "Jill?

What about you?"

"Yeah, if you're offering."

"Florence, what would you like?"

"An egg and soldiers, please."

While Jack started on the breakfast, Florence and I took a seat at the table.

"Florence, you haven't forgotten that I'm taking you to Candlefield this morning, have you?"

"What will we do when we get there?"

"I thought we could go to Cuppy C first, to see the twins."

"That's a funny name for a shop."

"I suppose it is."

"Can I have a bun there?"

"If you're a good girl. The twins have lots of yummy cakes to choose from."

"Can I have a milkshake too? A strawberry one?"

"I would think so. When I told the twins that you were going over there, they said they'd bring their little girls into the shop to see you. Do you remember Lily and Lil?"

"I think so."

"You were only three when they came over here. After we've been to Cuppy C, we'll go to Aunt Lucy's house. Do you know who lives with Aunt Lucy, Florence?"

"Is it her husband?"

"Well, yes, Uncle Lester lives there too, but Aunt Lucy also has a dog."

"Like Buddy?"

"No, not really. He's much bigger than Buddy."

"He doesn't growl, does he, Mummy? I don't like dogs that growl."

"No, Barry's a big soft thing. I think you'll like him."

"That's a funny name for a dog."

"He isn't the only animal that Aunt Lucy has at her house."

"Does she have a cat too?"

"Not a cat. Can you think of an animal that has a shell?"

"A tortoise?"

"That's right. She has a tortoise called Rhymes."

"That's a funny name too. Can I play with him?"

"Tortoises don't really like you to play with them, but you can definitely talk to him."

"When are we going to Candlefield?"

"I have to go out for a little while first, but as soon as I get back, we'll go over there."

"And then it will be freaky time, won't it, Mummy?"

"This afternoon, yes."

Jack's fry-up certainly hit the mark. After I'd finished, I went upstairs to shower and get dressed.

"Right, you two, I won't be long." Buddy was practically climbing my legs now. "Jack, can you feed this dog. I think he might be hungry."

"Will do. Be careful at Tweaking Manor."

"I will. See you later."

***

When I arrived at the manor house, Elizabeth Judge's car was already parked in front of the house. It was she who greeted me at the door.

"Jill, come in, we're in the dining room."

The fire had been lit, so the room was much warmer than on my last visit. At the head of the table was

Caroline, who looked much better than when I'd seen her the day before.

"How are you feeling, Caroline?"

"Much better, thank you. I'm still a little unsteady on my feet, but I'm getting there, slowly but surely."

"Once the drugs that Ransom was feeding her are out of her system, she'll be fine," Elizabeth said. "Do take a seat, Jill. I'll go and make a cup of tea."

Elizabeth disappeared out of the room, and I took a seat next to Caroline.

"It's a pity I didn't listen to Elizabeth earlier," she said. "She told me she suspected that Ransom was behind all of this Mulgrave business, but I didn't want to believe it. He's always been a bad lot, but I never thought he was capable of something like this. What about you, Jill, are you alright? I'm surprised you managed to overpower him. Ransom is a big man."

"I'm fine. I can handle myself. How is Ransom? Have you heard?"

"He's out of hospital and in police custody. He has some bruising to the head, but no permanent damage."

Elizabeth came back into the room, handed out the tea, and then joined us at the table. "I have a few questions for you, Jill, if that's alright?"

"Sure. Fire away."

"How did you find the secret passageway that leads out under the back garden?"

"I'd love to be able to tell you that it was great detective work, but the truth is, it was pure luck. I sneaked into the house on Friday night, to check on Caroline. On my way back out, I saw Ransom, and curiosity got the better of me. I followed him, saw him open the wall that led into the secret passageway, and managed to slip in behind him."

"What do you think actually happened between Ransom and Mulgrave?"

"Unless Ransom decides to confess everything, we may never know. I'm pretty sure Mulgrave had known about the secret passageway and vault for some time, perhaps even years. Since he discovered its whereabouts, he's been trying to open the vault, but without the combination, it was a hopeless endeavour. That's the reason he went for a walk most evenings. He didn't want to use the entrance inside Tweaking Manor in case he was seen, so he used the one at the far side of the grounds. That would also explain why he didn't leave your employment when you cut his wages. A butler, with his wealth of experience, could easily have walked straight into another job, but he didn't want to leave Tweaking Manor while there was still a chance that he might get his hands on the treasure in the vault."

"How did Ransom get involved?" Caroline asked.

"It all started on the night of your birthday when he was playing billiards with Dominic. He'd had a few drinks and knocked the goblet onto the floor. The base dislodged and Ransom saw a series of numbers engraved inside. He obviously thought it was the combination to the vault. He must have heard the rumours that Mulgrave knew the whereabouts of the vault, so he approached him and struck a deal. Mulgrave would take Ransom to the vault, and Ransom would use the numbers he found to open it. But once Mulgrave had shown him the vault, Ransom no longer needed him."

"So he killed him and made it look like suicide?"

"I believe so. Then he planted the goblet in Mulgrave's

room to provide a motive for him taking his own life."

"The whole affair is beyond dreadful," Caroline said. "I feel terrible about what happened to Mulgrave. He was wrong not to tell us about the vault, but he didn't deserve to die in that way."

"What will you do now that you know the whereabouts of the vault?"

"There's not much we can do without the combination," Elizabeth said.

"Couldn't you bring in someone to crack it open?"

"We'll definitely investigate that possibility, but given its whereabouts and construction, it would probably cost a small fortune to get inside it, and neither of us believes there's likely to be anything of value in there. Our current financial situation is bad enough without spending money on a fool's errand."

**

I'd asked Jack to take Buddy for a walk so that I could be alone with Florence when I magicked us over to Candlefield for the first time. Needless to say, Buddy had shown the usual degree of enthusiasm for the walk, and Jack had practically had to drag him out of the front door.

"How do we get to Candlefield, Mummy?" Florence said. "Do we catch a bus?"

"No, darling, we have to use magic to get there."

"But, Mummy, you haven't shown me that spell."

"That's okay, darling. I'll magic us both over there."

"How?"

"It's very simple. Just hold my hand and the next thing you know, we'll be there."

"Will it make me dizzy?"

"No, you'll be fine. Take Mummy's hand." She hesitated for a moment, but then put her little hand in mine. "Okay, I'm going to count to three, and then we'll go. Are you ready?"

"Yes."

"One, two, three. And here we are."

Florence looked around. "Is this Candlefield, Mummy?"

"Yes, darling, this is Cuppy C. Look, the twins are over there, behind the counter."

"Hi, Florence," Pearl shouted.

"Yoohoo." Amber waved.

The twins' daughters appeared from behind the counter.

"I'm Lily." She gave Florence a hug.

"I'm Lily too." Lil joined in the hug-athon.

I shot Amber a puzzled look.

She shrugged. "Lil has decided to call herself Lily."

"Right." That wasn't going to be at all confusing.

"Would you like something to drink, Florence?" Pearl said.

"Mummy said I could have a strawberry milkshake."

"In that case, I'd better get you one."

"What about something to eat, Florence?" Amber pointed to the display in front of her. "We have lots of tasty buns."

Florence stuck her nose on the glass and studied them. "Could I have the pink one, please?"

"The strawberry cupcake? Of course you can. If that's alright with your mummy."

"That's fine." I nodded. "And could I get a caramel latte and a blueberry muffin, please?"

The two Lilys chose their drinks and cakes, then the three kids went to sit at a table in the corner.

"Florence gets more beautiful every time I see her," Pearl said. "She must get it from Jack."

"Cheeky mare." I glanced over at the three girls. "They seem to have hit it off."

"I knew they would."

"I'm going to take Florence to see Aunt Lucy when we're finished here. Do you want me to take the girls with us?"

"There's no need," Pearl said. "We've asked a couple of the staff to come in so we can all spend some time together. They should be here in about twenty minutes."

"Great."

"I assume you've heard Mum's big news?" Amber said.

"What news? I haven't spoken to her today."

"She's only gone and won first prize in Candlefield in Bloom."

"What? How did she manage that? The last time I was over there, someone had dug up her flower bed."

"No idea. We only heard about it ourselves this morning. She didn't go into any detail, but she's on top of the world, and she said she was looking forward to seeing you and Florence later."

Daze and Blaze walked into the shop.

"Do you have a minute, Jill?" Daze said.

"Sure."

She turned to Blaze. "Get me my usual, would you?"

"What did your last slave die of?"

"He didn't. You're still alive and well." Daze chuckled to herself as she and I made our way to a table near the window.

"That's my little girl, Florence, over there." I pointed. "With the twins' girls."

"Does she come over to Candlefield often?"

"This is her first visit, but she'll probably be over here regularly from now on."

"She's beautiful. She must take after her dad."

"Why does everyone keep saying that?"

"I'm only joking."

"What did you want to talk to me about, Daze?"

"I just wanted to say a big thank you for all the help you've given us recently. Romeo is due in court next week and you can bet he's going to get the book thrown at him this time. How did you manage to track him down?"

"I played a hunch. I talked to the guy who robbed Washbridge Bank with him. He wasn't too forthcoming at first, but after I'd told him that Romeo had done this several times before, he opened up to me. He told me that Romeo had used a dating agency in Washbridge, so I got in touch with Hilary at Love Spell. One of her assistants recognised his photograph and they arranged for me to go on a date with him. The rest you already know."

"Brilliant."

"What's happening on the elf case?"

"We've shut down the shop in Washbridge, and the two wizards responsible will be in court next week. They're going to be looking at some serious jail time. We've also caught the wizards who were running the operation at this end. The ones who were snatching the elves off the street in and around the sports centre."

"That's good news, but I can't help but feel sorry for all those elves who have been turned into charms."

"I have some good news there too."

"Oh?"

"Our people did some tests on the charms and they discovered the silver gunk didn't actually kill them. It just put them in a state of suspended animation."

"Does that mean they're still alive?"

"Yes, and we've already managed to remove the gunk from all those who were in the cabinets in the shop."

"How are they?"

"They're going to need bed rest, but the doctors say they should be okay. Once they've fully recovered, they'll reverse the effects of the Shrinkometer."

"What about those elves that had already been sold and are on charm bracelets?"

"We've got that covered too. We managed to recover the sales ledger from the shop, so we have the names and addresses of all the people who bought charms. There's a big undercover operation in progress as we speak."

"Doing what?"

"We've recruited a large number of witches and wizards who are going to visit all the addresses in the sales ledger, to try and recover the charms."

"That's fantastic news."

Blaze appeared at the table. "You owe me five pounds, Daze."

"Put it on my account. I was just thanking Jill for all the help she's given us."

"Yeah, thanks, Jill." Blaze took a seat next to me. "If you can just sort out the A-juice case, we'll be able to put our feet up for a few days."

"You mentioned that before. What exactly is A-juice?"

"Acorn juice."

"I didn't realise there was such a thing."

"The demand for it here in Candlefield far outstrips the supply, so gangs of shapeshifters collect the acorns from Washbridge and bring them back here to extract the juice. They're making a small fortune."

"Are you making any progress?"

"None so far. These gangs are notoriously difficult to track down. They look just like real squirrels. The only thing that gives them away is their behaviour."

"How so?"

"They're very protective of the territory they're farming, and they're quite prepared to use violence to keep intruders away."

"Such as throwing acorns at them?"

"Exactly."

"In that case, I might just be able to help you find them."

Chapter 25

Florence had clearly hit it off with the two Lilys. The three of them were chatting, giggling and generally having a whale of a time. The only issue was that Florence was clearly struggling a little with the name situation. Every time she said *Lily*, the other two both responded.

Once the two assistants had arrived and taken over behind the counter, we rounded up the girls and made our way to Aunt Lucy's house. Florence and the two Lilys ran a few yards ahead.

"Amber, how come Lil is calling herself Lily now?"

"She came home from school one day and said she was fed up of being called Lil because some of the other kids were calling her Lil Lil. She announced there and then that she wanted to be called Lily."

"Are you okay with that?"

"Of course I am. As long as she's happy, I don't mind. I should've stuck to my guns and called her Lily when she was born. It would've saved all this messing around."

"Fair enough. I still don't understand how Aunt Lucy's garden won the competition. When I saw it, it was in a terrible mess."

"Maybe all the other entries were rubbish too," Pearl said.

"Her next-door neighbour's garden is beautiful. Even if all the other entries were pants, I would still have expected him to win."

"I guess we'll soon find out."

Aunt Lucy was looking through the front window. As soon as she spotted us, she came running out of the house, took all three of the girls into her arms, and gave them a great big hug.

"It's so lovely to see all three of you together at last. Are you having fun, Florence?"

"Yes, thank you, Aunt Lucy. Lily and Lily are my best friends here in Candlefield."

"That's lovely. I have cake and pop inside for you."

"I'm full, Aunt Lucy." Florence rubbed her tummy. "I had a milkshake and a bun in Cuppy C."

"What about you two?"

The two Lilys couldn't eat another crumb either.

"Sorry, Grandma."

"That's okay. Come on in. Barry's waiting to meet you, Florence."

"He won't growl at me, will he?" Florence was clearly still a little nervous.

"Barry? No. He's a big soft thing. Come on. I'll introduce you to him."

Florence was soon stroking Barry, who was on his best behaviour. Aunt Lucy had no doubt warned him that he mustn't jump up around the little girls.

"Barry's a lot bigger than Buddy, isn't he, Mummy?"

"He is, and he has a lot more hair too." I turned to Aunt Lucy. "What's this the twins tell me about you winning the Candlefield in Bloom competition?"

"I did indeed." She beamed. "Wait there." She nipped into the lounge and came back a few moments later, holding a small silver trophy. "And here's the proof."

"That's fantastic, but how did you manage it? The last time I was here, the flower bed had been wrecked."

"Why don't you all come and see for yourselves?"

She led the way through the house and out into the back

garden.

"Wow!" I was gobsmacked to see that the flower bed was back to its former glory. "How did you manage to do that so quickly?"

"I didn't. I woke up yesterday morning and it was like that."

"If you didn't do it, who did?"

"I don't know, but I suspect it was Charlie from next door. He's such a good sort. I think he must have come over and worked on it during the night. He's such a selfless man because if I hadn't won the competition, I'm sure he would've taken first place. As it turned out, he came second."

"Have you asked him if he did it?"

"I haven't had the chance. I've been around there a couple of times, but he wasn't in. I think he must have gone away, which is a little surprising because he'd been really looking forward to the competition."

Florence's first visit to Candlefield had been a resounding success. She'd made two new friends in Lily and Lily, and even Barry had won her over. But the highlight of the visit was when Rhymes had presented her with a poem, which he'd written especially for her.

When it was time for us to go home, Florence didn't want to leave, but I promised that we would make regular visits to Candlefield. After giving Aunt Lucy and the twins a kiss, she said goodbye to Lily, Lily and Barry, then she took my hand, and I magicked us back to the old watermill.

"Daddy!" She ran into the lounge where Jack was on the sofa. "Candlefield is brilliant." She jumped onto his lap, crumpling the newspaper he'd been reading. "I made two new best friends called Lily and Lily."

"That's lovely, darling, but I thought one of the girls was called Lil?"

"No, silly, they're both called Lily."

Jack shot me a puzzled look.

"Lil decided she wanted to be called Lily," I said, by way of explanation.

"Barry's much bigger than Buddy, Daddy."

"Is he nice?"

"Yes, he's really friendly. We were playing with him in the back garden. And Rhymes wrote a poem for me. Would you like to hear it?"

"I—err—"

"Of course he would," I chimed in. "Daddy loves Rhymes' poetry."

She took the sheet of paper out of her pocket and read out loud.

Florence is a pretty girl,
Who's very clever as well,
The only thing that would make her better,
Is if she had a shell.

"Do you like it, Daddy?"

"It's really great. It sounds like you had a lovely time in Candlefield."

"I did." Her face fell a little. "I wish you could come with us, Daddy."

"So do I, darling, but it's alright. I don't mind. As long as you enjoy yourself, that's all that matters."

"Mummy says we can go back there again soon." She jumped out of his lap. "Is it time to go freaky now?"

"Not yet, darling," I said. "Freaking Tweaking doesn't start until after lunch."

She gave me a puzzled look. "But we've been in Candlefield for ages."

"Don't you remember what I told you? When we go to Candlefield, the time here doesn't change."

"Why?"

"No one really knows. When we left here, it was ten o'clock. It's only five past ten now."

"That's silly. How long is it until freaky, then?"

"A couple of hours."

"That's ages." She sighed.

"It isn't all that long, and it will give me time to teach you a new spell. Would you like that?"

"Yes, please." Her face lit up. "Which spell can I learn?"

"I'm going to teach you the 'grow' spell."

"Will that make me grow so I'm as big as you and Daddy?"

"No, darling, that's not what the 'grow' spell does. It makes plants grow taller."

"Can we do it now?"

"Yeah, let's go into the garden."

On our way out of the lounge, I grabbed the spell book. Buddy was fast asleep on his bed and he didn't stir as we walked past him. Out in the garden, Florence walked around, looking at the various flowers.

"Which one shall we make grow, Mummy?"

"You can choose."

"This one."

"The yellow pansy?"

"Yes, please."

"Okay, come and sit on the step next to me and we'll

look at the spell together." Once she'd joined me, I opened the spell book at the appropriate page. "You have to remember all of these pictures to cast the spell."

"There's a lot, Mummy. I don't think I can remember all of them."

"You will. Just keep practising until you get it right. Okay?"

"I'll try." She studied the page, looking at each picture in turn. After a few minutes, she said, "I think I know them now."

"Okay, why don't you give it a try." She put the book down on the step and walked over to the pansy. "Now, close your eyes and think about each picture in turn."

"I have to focus too, don't I, Mummy?"

"That's right. That's the most important part."

She screwed up her eyes really tight and after a few seconds, opened them again.

Nothing had happened.

"It didn't work, Mummy."

"Don't worry. Maybe you got the pictures in the wrong order or forgot one of them. Why don't you take another look at the spell book?"

"Okay." She came back to the step, picked up the book and studied the spell for a few more minutes. "I think I know it now."

"Okay, give it another try."

She closed her eyes again and within a few seconds, the pansy started to grow.

"It's working, Florence, but don't open your eyes yet or it will stop growing. I'll tell you when to open them."

I waited until the pansy had grown to twice its original height. "Okay, you can open your eyes now."

"Look, Mummy! Look how big it is."

"Good job!" I gave her a kiss. "Aren't you a clever little witch?"

"Can I do it to another flower, Mummy?"

"Okay, why don't you try the one next to it?" She did, and this time it worked first time. "Very good. That'll do for today. Why don't you go upstairs and play for a while and then, after lunch, we'll go to Freaking Tweaking?"

***

Jack, Florence and I had a light lunch of sandwiches. We'd just finished eating when Kathy and Lizzie arrived. I could see straight away that Lizzie wasn't her usual bubbly self, so when she'd gone through to the garden with Florence, I asked Kathy what was wrong.

"It's that stupid charm bracelet of hers."

"Is she still bugging you to buy her some more charms?"

"No, it's not that. They've disappeared."

"*Disappeared*?" I acted suitably surprised. "What do you mean, *disappeared*?"

"It's the weirdest thing. When she woke up this morning, the bracelet was still there, but all the charms had gone."

"Stolen, you mean? Did someone break in?"

"There's no sign of a break-in, and nothing else has been taken. Those charms are ridiculously expensive, but it's not like they're solid silver. They're not worth anything. And why not take the bracelet? Why just the charms?"

"That is weird. Is it possible she lost them and doesn't

want to tell you?"

"I thought the same thing at first, but it's happened to her friends too. She's spoken to several of them this morning, and they've all lost their charms. It's the strangest thing I've ever seen."

After Florence had fed Buddy, we all made our way to Tweaking Meadows, which was just outside the village. The area had been completely taken over by the carnival. In addition to all the usual rides, there were lots of stalls, including the obligatory hook-a-duck. There was no shortage of food stalls too, although you would have struggled to find anything remotely healthy.

Kathy came up with a great idea.

Yes, I was surprised too.

She suggested that one of us should accompany the girls while the other two grabbed a rest and a cup of tea. The plan was that we'd each take a shift. Jack volunteered to go first, so Kathy and I queued at the refreshments stall where we bought what was laughingly described as tea, but which resembled and tasted like lukewarm dishwater.

"Thank goodness it was the carnival today," Kathy said. "It seems to have taken Lizzie's mind off her charm bracelet."

"She seems to be having fun. They both do. I was surprised when Jack told me that Mikey had gone go-karting with Peter. I thought he'd given up on that."

"He had, but Pete managed to persuade him to give it another go. Mikey does enjoy it once he's there, but it's not cool to be seen doing anything with your parents."

When Jack came back, it was my turn to accompany the kids.

"Okay, you two. What would you like to do next?"

The kids dragged me to the ring-toss stall where you had to throw a hoop over a soft toy to win it. As always with these stalls, it was clearly fixed, but a little magic ensured both of the girls came away with a teddy bear, much to the consternation of the stall owner. Next, we went on the dodgems. Florence shared a car with me while Lizzie drove her own. I wasn't sure if Florence would like it, but the more we crashed into other cars, the more she whooped with delight. The kids wanted to go on the helter-skelter next, but the guy in charge said they'd had to close it because of the high winds that had started to gust since we arrived.

When my time was up, I took the kids back to the refreshment stall, and Kathy took over. When she'd gone, Jack said, "Do you know anything about those charm bracelets?"

"I do, actually. Those charms were real elves. They'd been abducted from Candlefield, dipped in silver gunk and then shrunk."

"That's awful."

"I know. Luckily, the scientists in Candlefield have found a way to reverse the effects. Daze's people have been retrieving the charms from the human world, so they can rescue the elves. It's a bit hard on poor old Lizzie and her friends, but it's for the best."

It was only a few minutes later when Kathy came back to join us.

"Hey, your time isn't up yet." I tapped my watch.

"They're closing the carnival because of the high wind, so I bought the kids some candy floss to make up for it."

"It's yummy, Mummy." Florence held it out to me. "Try

some."

Before I could decline, a gust of wind blew the stick of candyfloss out of her hand, and onto my face.

"Yuk!" Although I managed to pull the stick away, most of the candy floss was still stuck to my face and hair.

Jack, Kathy and Lizzie were in hysterics.

"It's not funny!"

Florence clearly didn't think so either because her bottom lip began to quiver. "I don't have any candyfloss left."

"It's alright, pumpkin." Jack put his arm around her. "We'll go and get you some more before they close."

"Yes, thanks, I'm fine," I said while pulling candyfloss from my hair. "Thanks for asking."

"Why don't you shoot off home and wash your hair," Jack said. "We won't be long."

"We should be making tracks, too." Kathy took Lizzie's hand.

"What happened to you?" Buddy began to roll around the floor, laughing. It was the first time I'd seen him crack a smile since he'd arrived.

Ignoring him, I made my way upstairs to the bathroom and decided it would be easier just to have a shower. It took ages to get all the candy floss out of my hair, but I eventually managed it. I was sitting on the bed, blow-drying my hair, when I heard Jack calling from downstairs.

"Jill, come down here. Quick."

I hurried down to find him in the kitchen, staring out at the garden. "What's wrong? Where's Florence?"

"That's what I'd like to know." He pointed to the lawn,

which was now over five feet tall. "She's out there somewhere with Buddy."

I stepped outside. "Florence, where are you?"

"Over here, Mummy." Her voice came from the far side of the garden.

"What did you do?"

"I've been practising the 'grow' spell."

"Stay where you are."

I reversed the spell, and little by little, the grass returned to its normal height.

"Sorry, Mummy. I think I did it for too long."

Chapter 26

It was Monday morning. I'd just kissed Florence goodbye, and I was on my way out of the door when Jack called me back.

"Jill, you haven't forgotten that it's the open day at the hotel this afternoon, have you?"

"I had, actually. We're not going, are we? It'll most probably be rubbish."

"We have to. I've already told Florence and she's looking forward to going."

"Okay. What time is it?"

"It starts at midday, but I thought we could go about four, after I've picked her up from school. Can you make it back home by then?"

"Yeah, I'll be here."

"Okay. See you this afternoon."

***

Mrs V had a plaster on her forehead and another one on the top of her ear.

"Oh dear. Are you okay, Mrs V?"

"No, I'm not. Those squirrels are getting more and more belligerent. I was sitting under the parasol, but they still managed to hit me with their acorns. Armi is furious about it. He's talking about getting a catapult."

"There's really no need for him to resort to that."

"That's easy for you to say, Jill. You're not the one under attack in your own back garden."

"That's true, but I happen to know quite a lot about squirrels."

"Do you?"

"Yes. Haven't I ever mentioned that I did a special project on them at school?"

"I don't think so."

"It was part of the biology curriculum back then. It's a little-known fact that squirrels' moods are affected by the moon's cycle."

"They are?"

"Absolutely. I'm confident you'll notice a marked improvement in their behaviour over the next few days as the moon phase changes."

"Are you sure about that?"

"Positive."

"I hope you're right." She clearly wasn't convinced. "Because if this continues, it will be the catapult for them."

"If you ask me," Winky said, "those acorns are affecting the old bag lady's brain. She's even nuttier than she used to be."

"As far as I recall, I didn't ask you. Anyway, how's the life coaching coming along?"

"Brilliantly. I should have got one years ago."

"What sort of things do you do?"

"Learn to set attainable goals, create action plans, find the right work-life balance, to name just a few."

"And you really think it's helped you?"

"I'm a different cat since I started doing it. You should give it a try."

"Me? Do you really think so?"

"Definitely. Let's be honest, your life's a mess."

"That's not true."

"Of course it is. You stumble from one disaster to another."

Harsh, but quite possibly true.

"I'll think about it."

"While you're doing that, how about some salmon?"

"You're on a ban, remember?"

"Not anymore." He waved a sheet of paper in front of me.

"What's that?"

"This is the name and address of the person who's been hacking the old bag lady's account."

"Already?"

"Nobby doesn't hang around."

"Let me see." I grabbed the paper from him. "Is he sure about this?"

"One-hundred percent. Nobby doesn't make mistakes."

"Okay."

"Come on, then. Let the cat see the salmon."

"Coming right up."

Around mid-morning, Mrs V popped her head around the door to inform me that Mr Edwards was here to see me.

"Send him in, would you?"

I was a little taken aback when he walked through the door because his white hair was now bright red. He'd clearly been at the hair colouring.

"Thanks for seeing me, Jill." Rusty ran his fingers through his hair. "What do you think of it?"

"It looks — err — good."

"I think so too. It's made me feel twenty years younger."

"Good for you."

"I won't stay long, but I have some good news that I wanted to share with you."

"What's that?" As if I didn't already know.

"I had a visit yesterday from the man who lives across the park."

"The man you saw at the window, you mean?"

"That's right. He was accompanied by the woman who shot him."

"What?" Another Oscar-worthy performance from me.

"Don't worry. It turns out I'm not a crazy old man after all. I really did see what I thought I saw. Apparently, they'd been rehearsing for a play."

"But I thought you said the woman in the park wasn't the same woman you saw doing the shooting?"

"I — err — must have been mistaken about that."

"Right. I wonder why Mr and Mrs Smart didn't tell the police they'd been rehearsing for a play."

"I have no idea."

"It sounds like there's something funny going on."

"I don't think so. I'm sure it's all above board."

"Perhaps I should pay them another visit?"

"No, don't do that. Better to forget the whole incident. I just thought I'd let you know, and thank you again for all your help."

"It was my pleasure, Rusty. I'm glad it's all been cleared up."

Just as I'd expected, Rusty was far too much of a gentleman to tittle-tattle and tell me that the woman he'd seen wasn't the man's wife. Not long after he'd left, Mrs V came through to my office again.

"Jill, now that the Tweaking Manor case is closed, shall I prepare the invoice?"

"No, don't bother. I'm not going to bill them."

"Why not?"

"The financial situation over at Tweaking Manor is dire; it looks like they're going to lose the house. An invoice from me is only going to add to their misery."

"Are you sure?"

"Absolutely. Just mark the case closed, please."

As soon as she'd left the room, Winky jumped onto my desk.

"Are you insane?"

"What do you mean?"

"Why aren't you going to invoice the Tweaking woman? You did the work, didn't you?"

"Yes, the goblet has been found and a man has been arrested for the murder of the butler."

"And you found the secret vault too, didn't you?"

"Yes, but that's no good to Caroline because no one knows the combination. All they have is an old parchment that doesn't make any sense."

"Do you have a photo of it?"

"The parchment? Yeah, why?"

"Show it to me."

"What good would that do?"

"It can't do any harm, can it?"

"I guess not." I took out my phone and flipped through the photos. "This is the goblet, that's the vault, and this is the parchment. You can just about read the legend."

"Give it here." He'd snatched the phone before I had chance to object.

"It's obvious, isn't it?" he said.

"What's obvious?"

"The combination to the vault of course."

"If you're talking about those numbers engraved inside the goblet, it isn't those. We tried them."

"Of course it isn't. That's clearly just a serial number."

"Then what do you mean?"

"Look at the legend printed on the parchment. The answer is right there in front of you."

"I've read it a thousand times. It just says the first one to unlock the vault will find riches beyond their wildest dreams. How does that help?"

"That's *not* what it says."

"Yes, it is."

"*No*, it isn't. It actually says the first one to unlock the vault."

"Same difference."

"No, it isn't."

"I have no idea what you're talking about, Winky."

"Look at the goblet again."

"I've seen it a million times. It's an ugly thing."

"Look at the engraving."

"You just said yourself that's only a serial number."

"I don't mean the serial number. I'm talking about the names on the goblet."

"They're all the previous owners of Tweaking Manor dating back to when it was first built."

"Look at the first name on the list."

"Rudolph Tweaking. What about him?"

"What's engraved next to his name?"

"His date of birth and death."

"Bingo!"

"Hold on. Are you saying — ?"

"That's the combination. It's obvious."

"It can't be that simple." I took the phone back from him. "Someone must have thought of that already."

"Apparently they didn't."

I made a call to Tweaking Manor. Elizabeth Judge answered.

"Hi, Elizabeth, it's Jill. Look, this is a really long shot and I'm probably wasting your time. I've just reread the legend on the parchment, and it occurred to me that it might refer to the first lord of the manor, Rudolph Tweaking."

"Really?"

"I could be wrong. I probably am, but it might be worth trying his date of birth. Or death. Or both? What do you think?"

"It's definitely worth a try. I'll go and do it now."

"I'll stay on the phone, shall I?"

"There's no point, Jill. There's no reception down in the passageway. I'll nip down there now and give you a call back."

"Okay."

"So?" Winky blew on his claws. "Am I a bona fide genius or what?"

"We'll soon find out."

About twenty minutes later, my phone rang.

"Jill, you were right!" Elizabeth gushed. "It was his date of birth. The vault is open."

"Is there anything inside?"

"It's full of gold bars. Dozens of them. They must be worth an absolute fortune. Thanks to you, it looks like we'll be able to save the house. How did you realise that was the combination?"

I glanced at Winky. "It just sort of came to me."

"We can't thank you enough, Jill. I'm in the dining room with my sister. She says that when you submit your invoice, she's going to pay you a big bonus. A very big bonus."

"There's really no need."

"There absolutely is. You've just saved Tweaking Manor. Thank you so much. Just a second, my sister is saying something. She says that when the house has been renovated, we'd love for you and your family to come and stay for a few days, to see it in its full glory."

"That would be lovely. I'll look forward to it."

When I'd finished on the call, Winky was looking very smug indeed. "It's not often I'm wrong, but I was right again, wasn't I?"

"You were."

"Sorry? I didn't catch that."

"I said you were right."

"Again?"

"Again."

"Did I hear that you're going to get a very big bonus?"

"That's what she said."

"Which of course, you'll be sharing with me."

***

I'd finished work early because I wanted to be home in time to accompany Jack and Florence to the open day at the revamped hotel. First, though, I had another call to make.

"Yes?" snapped the woman who answered the door. "I

don't buy at the door, and I'm watching my favourite soap."

"Don't you remember me, Mrs Mizus?"

"Err, no. Should I?"

"We met when you paid Annabel Versailles a visit a few days ago."

"Oh yes. Sorry. Julie, wasn't it?"

"Jill, actually."

"How did you know where I live? Did Annabel ask you to pay me a visit? Is she okay?"

"Healthwise, she's fine, but she'd be a lot better if you stopped hacking her YarnAgram account."

Her cheeks flushed. "I—err—have no idea what you mean."

"The game is up, Maud. The IP address that hacked the account was traced back to this address."

Do you like the way I said *IP address* as though I knew what I was talking about? Good, eh? Winky had asked Nobby the Nerd to talk me through it.

"I—err—"

"Don't waste your breath trying to make excuses. I can already guess what happened. You knew how popular Mrs V is in the yarn community. That's why you did your best to dissuade her from going online. When you discovered she'd opened a YarnAgram account, and saw how quickly she was amassing followers, you could see your crown slipping away, so you decided to sabotage her. How am I doing so far?"

"Does Annabel know?"

"Not yet."

"Please don't tell her. I'm really sorry."

"Sorry doesn't cut it. If you don't want me to tell her,

you'd better remove all your posts from her account before the end of the day."

"Okay. I'll take them down."

"Then, you're going to follow Mrs V's account."

"Alright."

"And from now on, you're going to share all Mrs V's posts with all your followers."

"But, I—"

"Or I tell Mrs V it was you."

"Okay, okay, I'll do it."

***

As it was pouring with rain, we drove the short distance from the old watermill to the hotel.

"Look what I've found, Mummy," Florence said from the back seat.

"Mummy's driving, darling." Jack turned around. "What is it?"

"I think it's about freaky." She passed Jack the crumpled flyer.

"Where did that come from?"

"Beats me." I shrugged, and quickly changed the subject. "Winky cracked the combination of the Tweaking Manor vault."

"*Winky* did?"

"Yeah, he's going to be unbearable for the next few days. Still, it's worth it because Caroline said she's going to pay me a big bonus."

"That's brilliant."

"I know and very timely too. Profits are down."

"You made a profit?"

"Almost, but let's not spoil the day by talking about that. There had better be a good spread at the hotel. I'm really hungry."

"Do you think there'll be many people there?" Jack said.

"I doubt it."

As it turned out, I was wrong. The function room where the event was being held was full. There were lots of familiar faces in the crowd, including Donna, her husband and Wendy. Olga, her husband and kids were there too. As were the Stock sisters (who was manning the shop?), scary Miss Drinkwater, and the vicar. As soon as Florence spotted Wendy, she asked if she could go over and talk to her.

"Yes, but you mustn't leave this room."

"I won't, Mummy."

"The food is magnificent," Jack said. "We'll definitely have to visit the restaurant when it's open."

He was right. It was top notch and there was plenty of it. "I bet it'll be expensive."

Florence came running over to us.

"Mummy, look at this!" She was holding a snow globe.

"You mustn't pick up the ornaments, darling."

"But look! There's a little man inside it."

"I'm sure there is, but you still shouldn't—" That's when I spotted him. Florence was right, there was a little man inside; he was thumping on the glass, and obviously shouting something, but I couldn't hear what he was saying.

"Jill?" Jack looked at the globe. "What is that?"

"I know him."

"Who?"

"The man in the snow globe."

"What do you mean, you know him?"

"It's Aunt Lucy's next-door neighbour, Charlie Roundtree." I turned to Florence. "Why don't you go and talk to Wendy?"

"What about the snow globe, Mummy?"

"I'll see to this."

"Okay." She ran back across the room to Wendy.

"Hello, you two." The familiar voice caught me by surprise.

"Grandma, what are you doing here? I thought the open day was for Middle Tweaking residents only?"

"It is. Oh, I see you found my snow globe."

"Did you do this?"

"Do what?"

"Put Charlie Roundtree inside the snow globe."

"Of course I did."

"Why?"

"I would have thought that was obvious. He wrecked Lucy's garden."

"Charlie did it? But he's been so friendly to Aunt Lucy."

"He just pretended to be when all the time, he was scheming to make sure that he won Candlefield in Bloom. When he realised he couldn't beat Lucy fair and square, he destroyed her garden during the night."

"How can you know that?"

"Because, Jill, I saw him do it."

"Just a minute. Was it you who repaired the garden?"

"Of course it was, but don't tell Lucy. I don't want people thinking I've gone soft."

"And then you put Charlie in here?"

"A fitting punishment, I thought."

"You can't keep him in there indefinitely."

"Of course not. Just for a few days. Or weeks."

"Hold on, did you just say you were a resident of Middle Tweaking?"

"That's right."

"Since when?"

"Since I bought this hotel of course."

Oh bum!

ALSO BY ADELE ABBOTT

The Witch P.I. Mysteries
(A Candlefield/Washbridge Series)

Susan Hall Investigates (A Candlefield/Washbridge Series)

Murder On Account (A Kay Royle Novel)

Web site: AdeleAbbott.com
Facebook: facebook.com/AdeleAbbottAuthor